CHINESE

TAKEAWAY

Ben Nevis & The Gold Digger

Book 3.

W0006089

CHAPTER 1

The Portuguese island of Madeira is a favourite holiday destination of the Brits. Sunshine, beaches, clear blue sea, wine, and superb local cuisine – what more could you want? Well, that isn't the Madeira I was sampling. It was dark, one o'clock in the morning, and I was crouched hidden in a thicket of thorns that had me in their grip, and let me know I wasn't welcome amongst them. The thicket was at the back of the Pico dos Barcelos viewpoint, a favourite place for holidaymakers to visit as it was a flat promontory that pushed out from the hillside three hundred and fifty metres above sea level, giving a panoramic view over the capital Funchal in the distance below, with the cruise ships' lights flickering at the dockside and the moonlight bouncing off the shimmering bay beyond. During the day the car park beside the promontory would be rammed, and the mobile drinks and ice cream sellers doing a roaring trade. At one in the morning, it was empty; I could see across the level concrete platform to the railings at the far edge, a favourite suicide hotspot for those poor people that the beauty of the island couldn't offer enough to save. One car stood in the car park and one man stood by the railings, his lonely figure silhouetted against the night sky; he was carrying a small oblong box.

Commander Clarence Woodward, head of MI6, had hired me and the Gold Digger – more about her nickname later – to follow this man and the box in London and to see where it would end up. He'd flown from Gatwick to Madeira, spent a night in an apartment in Funchal, and was now stood waiting in the darkness on a tourist viewpoint three hundred and fifty metres above the capital city. Woodward had given me a direct line mobile phone that was programmed to call him and only him; I'd checked in with him earlier when the man had led us to the promontory. Woodward thought it was probably going to be the place for a swap, the box for money. Stay with the box was the order.

My earpiece crackled into action. 'Visitors, two of,' Gold's voice warned me.

I pushed myself lower into the thicket and another two thorns took advantage and attacked my backside as I did so. I'd been in that damn thicket since nine that evening, having slipped in unnoticed as the last of the visitors took their final pictures of each other by the railings with the view behind and left for their hotels or cruise ships. All except our mark; he had stayed. At eleven I was beginning to think our information had been wrong and this wasn't the place where he was going to make the swap, but Woodward had been insistent that it was and so I had to stay. I heard the crunch of shoes on pebbles approaching from the car park at the same time as the mark did. He turned from the railings as two figures joined him; they shook hands.

'Two males,' Gold said over the earpiece. I couldn't tell from my position.

The muffled conversation between all three at the railings rambled on for a bit and then became heated; hands were being waved. One of the men was trying to take the box case from the mark; he was resisting. A fist swung. The mark slumped to the ground, lifeless. The two men talked, a decision was made, and they lifted him up and dropped him over the railings. He was dead, he had to be; the drop was pretty sheer, and a body bouncing off rocks all the way to the hard dry floor at the bottom two hundred and fifty metres below didn't stand a chance. This wasn't in the plan; the plan was to follow the box to wherever its final destination was and then retrieve it, and when well clear of that final destination to call in an unmanned Reaper Drone strike. Woodward hadn't said anything about murder, but in my line of work, moving in the circles I sometimes do, it's not uncommon

'The mark's been killed,' I told Gold through my radio mic clipped on my collar. 'They threw him over.'

'Over what?'

'Over the railings.'

'Christ!'

'They have the box.'

'They must have somebody coming to pick them up – they didn't leave a car in the car park, they walked in.'

'Maybe they have one parked a bit down the road. Time to go and get ahead of them.'

'Okay.'

I moved silently out of the thicket and stepped straight onto a tourist's discarded drinks can that crackled under my foot. They heard, they turned, they saw, and they reached inside their jackets. I didn't wait to find out what sort of guns they had; I sprinted across the car park and joined Gold as she emerged from the shadows at the gateway.

'Which way, or stay?' I asked Gold. We were both unarmed; this was supposed to be a *'follow and report'* job.

'This way.' She set off up the lane that led up the hillside. The tarmacked road for cars to drive up to the viewpoint ended at the gate, and from then on upwards it was just a dirt lane; hopefully the two killers would go down to wherever their car was on the road, and we'd be able to pick them up later and get back to trailing the box. They didn't go down; the *phut* of a gunshot from a gun with a silencer and a bullet hitting the dirt in front of me and sending up a puff of dirt said they were following. If they were military they'd be fit, and we had to find a way out of this situation as they'd be on us pretty quickly. We'd have to somehow reverse the situation, and that would probably mean killing them; and then Woodward would go bananas, and so would the Portuguese government.

A sign, *Nossa Senhora do Monte*, hung lopsided from a post pointing down a left hand track. I followed Gold down it for a couple of hundred metres as it wound between old whitewashed single storey houses that once belonged to goat herders and now served as holiday homes and Airbnb; some had lights on, and some had dogs that barked as we passed. The lane gave way to a rough courtyard at the back of a church, which we quickly skirted round to the wide front church steps that led down to a large open paved area. Gold seemed to know where we were, and I followed her down and saw our escape route: the famous Monte toboggan run. There they were, the wicker toboggans all roped up for the night at the top of the run; how many thousands of tourist bums had sat in those and sped down the narrow lanes of the hillside?

I love Gold; she knows exactly what she's going to do and she does it – no hesitation, straight in. She went to the front of the toboggans, knelt to take the eight inch knife from her ankle holster, cut the rope and pulled out the nearest one which, woken from its slumber, started to slowly move down the sloping concourse towards the run, followed by the rest.

'In, quick,' she said, jumping in.

I didn't need telling twice as I caught sight of our pursuers rounding the side of the church onto the front steps. I leapt in as our sled gained speed. The men who operate these sleds wear wooden clogs and hang on the back, moving their bodies from side to side to steer them; we didn't have a man on the back steering and were running free, and running faster all the time. Behind us, the other sleds freed from the rope gave in to the pull of gravity and started to follow us down, bumping the side walls of the lane and swinging round, with some coming down backwards and sideways. Our pursuers surely wouldn't follow? They did; I could see them in a sled in the moonlight, struggling in the middle of a mix of empty banging and barging toboggans a hundred metres behind us as we came to the first bend. It was a long one, and Gold pulled me over to join her leaning against the left side so that our weight somehow got us round, as I crouched ready to leap out if her steering had failed and we'd headed for the lane's edge and the drop into the valley below. Another straight fifty metres and I could see ahead in the moonlight another bend approaching, a sharp one; if we failed to get round this one, we'd shoot straight on over a verge at the side of the lane and into a low fence that had no chance of stopping us launching into the air above the valley and plunging to ground zero two hundred metres below.

'We won't make this one,' I shouted above the rumble of wood on stone, pointing ahead.

'We jump,' Gold shouted back. 'When I say so.'

The bend seemed to be coming at us faster and faster. I was poised with one foot on the bench seat in the sled, knee bent ready to launch myself out when the order came; beside me, Gold was in the same position. We watched as we bounced towards the corner.

'NOW!!' She shouted the order and we both leapt from the sled towards the opposite verge. I prepared myself for a hard landing, covering my face with my arms. It wasn't too bad – uncut long grass, not the thorny scrub I expected. I suppose the locals keep it nice for the tourists taking mobile phone videos on their journeys down.

I sat up and saw Gold kneeling a few feet away. She had been right, the sled hadn't made the corner; the low fence was gone, smashed down by the sled and on its way to the valley floor, followed by a train of toboggans nose to tail – or nose to nose, or tail to tail – leaping off the cliff edge in a line that reminded me of a passenger train going over the edge of a mountain that I'd seen in a movie at some time. Our pursuers didn't stand a chance; the bouncing mess of toboggans on the cobbled lane in front of theirs had obscured their sight of the upcoming corner, and we watched as too late they realised their fate and disappeared over the edge, box and all.

The rumbling of the wooden runners on the cobbles and the squeaking of the wicker toboggans hitting and rubbing against each other on their last journey gave way to an eerie silence as the last one went over.

'You okay?' asked Gold, standing up.

'Yes, pretty much. You?'

'Yes, fine.'

We walked to the broken fence and looked down. Far below us toboggans were scattered over the bottom of the valley, with some still bouncing slowly down where the hillside wasn't so steep to join them.

'See any life?' I asked Gold as we looked for our men.

'No.'

'I'm not going down to find that box. Needle in a haystack.'

'You won't need to.' She pointed down to the left. 'See the road?'

There was a narrow road coming from the left along the valley floor that reflected the moonlight, and slowly moving along it was a vehicle, side lights only; no dipped and no headlights, just side lights.

''Yes, got him,' I said. 'You think he's how they got up to the viewpoint?'

'Probably.'

The car flashed its headlights twice and stopped. A figure came out of the undergrowth further along the lane, and the car moved along and drew up alongside it.

'One made it,' I said.

The driver left the car and joined the figure. They moved into the dark of the undergrowth beside the road and came back out carrying a lifeless body.

'Number two,' I said. 'Looks like he didn't make it.'

'Can't tell from here, maybe just unconscious.'

The body was put into the car boot and both men got in and it drove off out of view. Meanwhile, behind us up the lane towards the church, voices were being raised and dogs starting to bark.

'Time to go,' I said and we started off down the lane, keeping to the side in as much cover as we could find. I'd made up my mind that whatever that box was, I wasn't going to die following it, and certainly not for the money Woodward was paying me. Gold and I were going home.

****

CHAPTER 2

The buzzing of a mobile woke me at my London apartment two days later. We'd flown out of Madeira later the same morning as the toboggan run. I took the next flight after Gold had taken one, just in case anybody had seen us on the hill and the authorities were looking for a couple who wrecked their main tourist attraction. The news of the wrecked sleds hadn't broken on the media by then, and our exit went smoothly.

The phone kept buzzing. It was the burner phone Woodward had given me for the job. I swung my legs over the side of the bed and rubbed the sleep from my eyes before answering him.

'Yes.'

'Eleven o'clock in the morning, Nevis, and you're still in bed. You should be ashamed of yourself.'

'Is that you, mother?'

He ignored the quip. 'I've read your email report on the Madeira fracas and also one from our Madeira Consulate – seems like you had some fun destroying one of their tourist attractions and killing a member of the Chinese Portuguese Embassy staff.'

'What, Chinese?' That shook me.

'Yes, according to the official report he was enjoying a view when the toboggans got loose and swept him over the edge. Unofficial report is that he was a diplomatic attache – that's the name we all use for our spies. Anyway, it has all been recorded as a terrible accident.'

'You didn't say anything about others being prepared to kill for that damn box – I could have been killed. And certainly not that the Chinese were involved. I wasn't armed, you said it was a straight forward follow and report job – nothing about armed assassins turning up. That box could be anywhere now.'

'It's mid-Atlantic, on its way to Rabat.'

'Morroco?'

'Yes, on board a freighter that left Funchal this morning.'

'How do you know that?'

'GPS.'

I realised what he meant. 'Sod you, Woodward, you had a GPS bug in that box all the time. So why was I following it if the bug would tell you where it was?'

'You were following it in case we had to get it back quickly, in case people we don't want to get hold of it *do* get hold of it.'

'Like the Chinese.'

He didn't answer the question. 'We need to meet, Nevis. I'll come over to your office this afternoon.'

'Like hell you will. I'm out, all day.'

'I've got a cheque for you.'

The bastard knew his way to my heart. 'Charing Cross, two o'clock.'

I snapped the phone off.

****

CHAPTER 3

Commander Clarence Woodward, my old boss when I was doing my ten years in the N14 section of the SAS, was now top dog – or one of the top dogs – in MI6, and I had unwittingly renewed our business relationship by getting mixed up in an illegal arms caper after being hired by a rich lady to kill her husband. Yes, I know what you are thinking, but the offer of a million quid was a lot more than I usually get as a private investigator, and made a nice change to following wayward husbands for rich wives, or wayward wives for rich husbands. To cut a long story short, the job turned out to be much more than a simple hit on the husband, and this lady was already on MI6's radar, and Woodward came out of the shadows and used Gold and me to sort it out. Since then, he's popped up now and again when he needs a job done that must not be traced back to MI6 if it goes tits up. If the worse comes to the worse, he and MI6 have never heard of me and I'm thrown to the wolves. Who needs enemies with friends like that? But the money's good.

I certainly wasn't going to have Woodward come to my small office in the Borough High Street, as he'd turn up with two bodyguards in long overcoats in a tinted glass car that would either shout 'drug dealer' or 'secret service' depending on who looked at it. The office was just a mail drop really; in my business you need a place registered as your business address with the SIA, and also for any mail. Most of my clients are referrals, and I meet them at a hotel or Simpsons for the advance cheque. My home address is in a serviced apartment block round the back of Waterloo overlooking Jubilee Gardens, with views of the Thames. It's rented in the name George Hadlow, a name I'd got off a cemetery plaque in a great plague burial ground off the York Road. I had become George Hadlow, with a GH driving license and other IDs, and the apartment was rented in GH's name, as was my Range Rover lease. Ben Nevis didn't exist on paper, and the only access to him was through the office which I seldom visited or the mobile number on the office door.

I called Gold. 'Woodward wants a meet at two at Charing Cross. You busy?'

'No, see you there at one thirty then.'

Alyson Gold: nicknamed the Gold Digger because of her tendency to purposely target older, wealthier men and relieve them of a good portion of their wealth by building a relationship that promised a life together sailing off shagging into the sunset, but always ended up shipwrecked on the rocks before leaving port, and always, but always, leaving the mark a lot less wealthy and the Gold Digger in possession of photos or videos that could send his marriage and social status onto the rocks as well. The marks never called in the law, never.

'One question, how did you know about the footpath from the viewpoint to the toboggan run? You been there before?'

'Flotilla 13, we had to do a quick in and out raid in Afghanistan against Isis in the Hindu Kush mountains and used sledges on the slopes for speed – had a week's training in Madeira during the off season, all hush-hush. Had a helicopter take us in from the Destroyer fifty miles away in the Atlantic and drop us at that viewpoint, then through the path to the slide and practice.'

I'd met Gold for the first time when she was a section head in Mossad and was in a backup Chinook on the Osama Bin Laden raid in Pakistan. I was in another Chinook with N14, and after the raid we were both debriefed and got to know each other. I went off to complete my ten years in N14 and was transferred to MI6, and she went off to join the elite Flotilla 13 group in Mossad, the group put together by Israeli Prime Minister Golda Meir that chased down and killed all the PLO Black September assassins that carried out the Munich Olympics massacre in 1972, which was way before Gold was seconded to them. They got them all in the end. We met up again in London many years after the Bin Laden affair, and after the Israeli police had cottoned onto her little money making scheme and chased her out of the country. She moved the UK and tried her Gold Digger routine on a client of mine and I rumbled it and confronted her. We recognised each other and hit it off. From then on she's been my back-up when needed, a sort of armed PA. She stays in the background on my jobs, but I know that if things go wrong she's there, ready to come in and help. She's my insurance policy. Scottish Widows don't do one like that.

I rang and booked an Uber for one o'clock.

****

On the concourse at Charing Cross Station is a British Rail cafe. When a job's running, I use it as a meeting place. From a window table you can see everybody approaching across the open concourse; a panoramic view, ideal. The food is rubbish, and the coffee is awful.

I'd bought two cups at one twenty-nine, knowing that Gold would be there on the stroke of one thirty. I'd only ever been late once for a meet with Gold, and the abuse hurled at me would have made a Swansea Docker blush. At precisely one thirty she sat down next to me, slipping off her shoulder bag and laying it on the table, open end towards us. That bag was our tool kit. Inside would be a communications unit, two Walther PKKs and 500 rounds of 9mm ammunition, a grenade, a flare, night vision glasses, and a basic medical kit. Be Prepared wasn't only the Boy Scouts motto, it was Gold's as well. To describe Gold is easy: for those of you of a certain age, just think Jennifer Rush singing The Power of Love; for those younger, go Google her.

'What's Woodward want? I'm not going back to Madeira for a while,' was her opening salvo.

'Me neither. That box had a GPS installed.'

She was silent for a few moments as she took that information on board. 'So why were we there?'

'In case it had to be retrieved quickly from people Woodward didn't want to have it.'

'Like people with guns that throw other people off viewpoints.'

'Could be, or the Chinese.'

'The Chinese?'

'Apparently one of our assailants that didn't abseil to the ground safely in his wicker basket was a Chinese Embassy man. For all we know, the other one may have been too.'

'Taking on the Chinese wasn't in the job description. How much are we getting?'

'Five grand a day, plus expenses.'

'No way, double it or I'm out.'

Now five thousand pounds a day between two of us plus expenses sounds a lot, yes? Well, it is if it's everyday, but in my line of work you don't work every day. I'm freelance, I work when I have work offered. If nobody comes into the office or phones with a job for London's top private eye – that's me in case you are wondering – then London's top private eye doesn't earn. So when I do work, I have to make enough to cover the barren times. My apartment is rented in case I have to leave quickly; I don't own anything traceable back to me. I don't know about Gold's home, wherever her home is – I have no idea, she won't tell me.

'You want a sandwich?' I offered.

'No, I want to know what's in that box that Woodward's letting run, and why it needs a chaperone ready to step in and rescue it.'

'He says it's on its way to Rabat now.'

'Are you kidding? That's the world centre for major crime – you got a stolen Monet to shift, then take it to Rabat, you've stolen the Crown Jewels, then there's a fence in Rabat. Ninety percent of the cocaine from the Afghanistan poppy fields comes through there. Dangerous place.'

'Nice beaches.'

'Bollocks to the beaches.' Gold had a direct way of letting you know her opinions.

'You're not keen then?'

'Money talks.'

She could be persuaded.

We passed a further ten minutes guessing the occupations of people who passed across the concourse in front of the cafe.

'International financier,' said Gold, as an obviously homeless old chap stopped to bend and pick up a cigarette end. 'They're having a hard time at present.'

'What a shame,' I said sarcastically.

'Junior Minister in Her Majesty's Government,' she said as a portly sixty year old in pin stripe suit hurried across. She looked at me with a smile. I took the hint.

'One of your clients?'

'Could be.'

That was a '*yes*'. I checked my watch.

'Woodward will be here soon.'

'Okay, give me a call later.' Gold gathered the shoulder bag and left, mixing into the commuter traffic on the concourse. I knew she wouldn't leave the station; she'd be somewhere around within sight of the café, just in case anything bad happened. Who knows, Woodward might be the subject of an assassination attempt. After all, we were at work, and her job was to watch my back; and she'd be doing just that.

Commander Clarence Woodward – Eton, Cambridge, Foreign Office and MI6 – came striding across the concourse to the cafe in his flowing fawn overcoat and brown bowler hat. You couldn't miss all six foot two of him, and the first time you see him the immediate impression is of a man from the Ministry. Who you *could* miss were his two bodyguards covering him. They'd be out there somewhere pretty close, but they were good, I couldn't spot them. No doubt Gold had.

'Good afternoon, Nevis,' he said, giving me a brusque nod as he removed his brown leather gloves and gave the seat a quick flap with them, in case any crumbs were lurking, before putting them on the table and sitting down.

'Coffee?' I offered.

'Good God, no – if committing suicide, I'd like to choose my own poison.'

'What's so important inside that box that people want to kill me?' Straight to the point, eh?

'Ah, well I'm afraid I can't tell you that = sort of top secret. All I can say is that if other terrorists knew it was out there, they'd all be after it like the Chinese are – especially Russia.'

'If whatever it is is that important, how the hell did it get *out there*?'

Woodward sat back and sighed. 'Well, there's always one bad apple in the barrel, Nevis – always one who's political views don't run parallel with our democratic ones.'

I sniggered.

'What are you sniggering about?'

'Well, the democratic views of your Eton and Oxford mates sitting on the front bench at

Westminster might not exactly run parallel with the democratic views of a single mother on benefits in a damp mouldy council flat in Hackney.'

'Nobody needs to live like that, Nevis – there are safeguards.'

'No doubt you had safeguards on the box – they didn't work either, did they?'

Woodward waved an end to the side track we were on. 'No, they didn't, so we have to get it back in sight, watch it, and then retrieve it.'

'We?'

'You and your Gold Digger lady. Why not, you've tracked it so far, yes? Carry on.' He pulled a copy of a photo from his inside pocket. 'Taken at Rabat port late yesterday afternoon.'

The photo was of a freighter at the dockside, with a series of photos of two men coming down the steps from the ship to the dock. The close-ups of the faces showed one to be Oriental and one of a Mediterranean appearance with a moustache. The box was under the Oriental one's arm.

'One of them, the Oriental gentleman,' Woodward continued, 'has a pronounced limp. Reading through your emailed report of the toboggan fiasco, he could be the one who got out of the debris and made it away in the car.'

I agreed, he could be. Probably was.

The last photo showed them going into a very plush hotel.

'Hotel Dar el Kabira', said Woodward. 'Bloody expensive, but just outside the Medina.'

'The Medina?'

'Very upmarket Brick Lane in the middle of Rabat – if you are selling or buying high end dodgy goods, there's a buyer or seller in the Medina, and probably more than one. But...' He paused for effect. 'What our two characters have for sale is well above the value of the Medina's usual items. No, I would think they've probably got a few meetings arranged in the hotel with prospective buyers, testing the water for a price. Keep the photos and find out who is offering to buy the box – get pictures of anybody having meetings with those two, send them through on my phone, and then we will decide when to retrieve it. Keep me up to date.'

'What aren't you telling me?'

'What do you mean?'

'Why Rabat? If the Chinese have got the box, why didn't they fly it to Beijing? Their Central Military Commission HQ is in Western Beijing, so why go to Rabat? What's there?'

He looked at me for a few moments as he decided whether to open up or not. He decided he had better, or I might walk away from the job. 'Casablanca. This week and next there is an International Arms Fair in Casablanca just sixty miles down the beach road from Rabat. We expect our Chinese friends to bus in interested buyers from there and hold some kind of auction. The Chinese we are dealing with are not from the Chinese Central Military Commission.'

'They're not?'

'No, they're MSS, Ministry of State Security, sometimes called the Guoanbu – basically they're the secret police and handle foreign intelligence. We believe they turned the chap they dumped over the railings in Madeira, and they know that what's in the box will be of considerable interest to all the UK's adversaries – all of them – so they can offer the relevant bits of interest to each country separately. So, we want to know who is interested in it, and then we want it back before they manage to get inside it'.

'Why haven't they opened it up already? If they know what's inside is so important, why not open it so others can see?'

'It's titanium, with a code lock nine-digit keyboard set into the top.'

'No problem cracking that.'

'No, but they also know the importance of the contents and would be afraid that any tampering might trigger an explosion to destroy the contents, or even worse an explosion and a nerve gas expulsion. The only safe way into the box is via the code lock, and they haven't got that. Yet.'

'Yet?'

'We suspect the victim on the viewpoint was one of a cell of spies, including one in the GCHQ building at Cheltenham. We haven't been able to identify him yet, but that's the home of the box and where it was stolen from. It's the only place that the information inside that box is kept and used. He was probably a minor employee, he hadn't access to it – somebody else is pulling the strings, which is why I want to know who the Chinese meet with. All clear now?'

'What's in the box?' I tried again.

'Keep in touch, Nevis.'

He stood and started to button his coat.

'No.' I shook my head and took a sip of my now cold coffee.

'What? What do you mean, *no*?' He leant towards me as though he hadn't heard right.

'Sit down.'

He sat back down and took in a deep breath. 'Money?' He knew me so well.

'Yes.'

He took another deep breath. 'Fifty thousand a week.'

'Eighty, there's two of us.'

'Oh yes, the Gold girl. Well, all right then, seventy-five and that's the limit. I could send the SAS, you know.'

'Seventy-five *and* expenses – and you can't send the SAS as you'd have to get approval from the Minister and the Ministry of Defence for that, and it sounds to me that whoever's democratic principles caused them to slip away with this *top secret* item and offer it to the market probably worked for the Ministry anyway, and so you can't take a chance that he had an ally in there with similar views who would soon let our friends in Rabat know the SAS were on their way and they'd disappear altogether with the box.'

He knew I was right. 'All right, seventy-five plus expenses – and if it goes belly up, Nevis, and you end up in some stinking foreign prison somewhere, you will be hung out to dry. We don't know you and have never heard of you. Any idea of a terrorist prisoner swap to get you back will be out of the question.'

'I'll need a parcel from the Consulate or Embassy or whatever we have over there in Morocco.'

'The Embassy is in Rabat.'

I smiled. 'Oh, that's handy – if it all goes tits up I can run in there.'

'Access would be denied,' he said, firmly returning my smile. 'Usual parcel, I take it?'

'Please.' The *usual parcel* was a sealed box with two Walther PKKs and 500 rounds of 9mm ammunition. You can't get guns through the modern airport sensors and metal detectors, so the easiest way to tool yourself up was with a parcel from the local Embassy once you were in place. Even if the host country opens the parcel they can't bring charges or do anything at all, as an Embassy parcel has diplomatic immunity inside or outside the country and should never be opened

'I'll be using the name Johnson.'

He nodded. 'Okay, have fun.' He rose again and picked up his gloves from the table and flicked the back of his coat. 'Can't you find a more suitable place to meet in future?' And he was gone. I waited a few minutes, left a pound on my saucer as a tip, and made my way out of the cafe. Behind me, the homeless chap Gold and I had watched pick up a fag end sidled up to the table and pocketed the coin. I smiled; perhaps he *was* an international financier on hard times after all. They seem to know where to find money when they want it, and he most certainly did.

I was still unsure whether Woodward had told me everything.

****

I wandered out of Charing Cross and up to St Martin's Lane. As this was a *'watch and report'* job I needed some 'eyes', and my *'go to'* man for all this kind of thing was Gilbert Charles. Gilbert has a gunsmiths in St Martin's Lane, and officially caters for the elite grouse shooting public school dickheads who take great joy in blasting young birds out of the sky in the name of sport. *Unofficially*, Gilbert, resplendent in his Prince of Wales check jacket, cavalry twill trousers, bow tie and brown brogues, is the top man for things like explosives, rented shotguns, fake IDs and passports, and other items that shouldn't really be on the market. He certainly looks the part of a county gent, with a large colour photo hanging on the wall behind the mahogany shop counter of him, a Springer with a grouse in its mouth, a 'broken' shotgun over his arm and a large Tudor country pile behind him. The photo had actually been put together by his own hand in the dark room he uses for developing fake ID photos at the back room of the shop. A fake ancestry family tree inscribed on parchment behind glass in mahogany frame hangs beside it, tracing Gilbert's blue blood back to 1066 with all of his ancestors being military officers. The only blue blood Gilbert has in him was from when an inmate in the Scrubs took offence at his false posh accent and stabbed him with a fountain pen. In reality his dad was a bookie's runner in Liverpool, and his mother a clippie on the Mersey buses. Anything of the family history before then is unknown; and as for living in a large Tudor mansion Gilbert has spent more time living at Her Majesty's Pleasure in various government 'mansions' around the country than he has as a free man. Like most of the con artists in our world, it's all smoke and mirrors.

The *antique* brass bell, made in India four years ago and now hanging inside the street door jangled as I went in. Gilbert looked up from reading the Racing News laying on the counter; business was slow.

'Ben!' He took off his reading glasses, 'How nice to see you.'

The warm welcome was because he knew I'd be spending some money. I don't make courtesy calls.

'Hello, Gilbert.' We shook hands. 'Not been closed down yet then?'

He laughed; he knew it was just banter. Gilbert and I go back a long time. I know what he does, and he probably guessed a long time ago what my profession is.

'What can I do for you this time?'

'I need a couple of walnuts. Ones I can get a clear picture with.'

Walnuts, for those of you who don't know the term within the surveillance arena, are not the edible type, but small cameras with a flat back that are the size of half a walnut. They link to a mobile phone by wi-fi, and the flat back has a plastic strip that pulls off to reveal a stick-on pad. You just pull the strip off, stick the *walnut* on a wall somewhere facing what you want to watch, and retire to anywhere within a hundred metres to view on your phone. Simple and effective. I handed Gilbert my mobile.

'Ten minutes,' he said, taking it and going into the back room. 'Don't nick anything,' he said, poking his head back round the door. 'I've got cameras watching.'

Cheeky bugger.

Ten minutes it was, almost to the second, when he emerged with a small paper bag and my phone.

'All set.' He opened the bag to show the two *walnuts*, not brown but a standard beige that would be unobtrusive stuck high on a wall. He turned on my mobile and showed me the operation. I already knew how to operate them, but a revision never hurt.

'Press the button on the *walnut*.' He took one out of the bag and pressed a small button on the side. 'One press for *on*, two for *off*, phone on, go to Apps, scroll down to this one,' He did that and showed me an app that looked like an open eye. 'Open it, and away you go.' He opened the app and held the *walnut* up, pointing it towards the street door which showed on the phone screen. 'Simple.' He double pressed the walnut button, put it back in the bag, clicked off my phone and gave both to me. 'Two hundred, anything else today, Ben?'

Not cheap, but when you consider an outside observation job could mean sitting in a car for hours, or hidden in a bush with rain and wind for company, a hundred pounds for a *walnut* that lets you sit in comfort somewhere within a hundred metres is well worth the money.

'No, that's it, Gilbert, thank you,' I said as I counted out three hundred in twenty pound notes from the grand I always keep with me; a good tip means a good immediate service next time. 'Take care, see you again no doubt.'

I turned to the door as it was opened from the outside, and a gentleman in similar attire to Gilbert came in.

'Mr Walsh, good afternoon, sir. Take a seat and I'll get your ammo from the back.' Gilbert turned to me as he held the door open for me to leave and gave a slight bow. 'Thank you so much, Lord Nevis. Do take care on the estate shoot, your Lordship, and do give my regards to her Ladyship.'

I kept a straight face as he offered a wink.

'Thank you, Gilbert, I will.' And I left. Smoke and mirrors, eh?

****

I gave Gold a call.

'I'm not here, leave a message or number and I'll call back.'

I didn't have to bother. She called back straight away.

'You have a tail.'

'What?' That was the last thing I expected her to say.

'Oriental gentleman, came in to the picture following Woodward at Charing Cross then swapped to you. Are you carrying? I think he is.'

'No.' I hadn't seen any reason to arm myself for a Woodward meeting.

'I am, I'll stay close.'

Why would the Chinese be on my tail? Not content with heating up the globe with their hundreds of coal powered power stations, filling the oceans with plastic and killing millions with COVID, now the bastards were after me! They'd tried to kill me and Gold in Madeira, so I didn't rate my chances in busy London, especially being unarmed. The game had suddenly changed from *track and trace* to a more serious *stay alive* and then track and trace. My mind set changed with it.

'Take him out.'

'You sure?'

'Yes, I'll go across into Trafalgar Square and we'll do a reverse round one of the fountains.'

'Okay.'

I crossed the road into the Square and chose the fountain in the far left corner, as it had the least people sitting round its edge. I gave a pound to a seed vendor for some pigeon food; I thought they'd been banned, but perhaps he sold what he could and did a quick bunk when the law approached. I made my way into the centre of the Square where there were less tourists and stopped to throw out the seed a little at a time, turning as I did so, as you would. I saw him: he'd stopped twenty metres away and was making like a tourist looking at a newspaper; the paper that would probably be held in front of him to shield the gun as he shot me. I couldn't see Gold. She's bloody good. I emptied the seed bag, screwed it up and popped it into a waste bin, before moving to the chosen fountain and starting to walk round it, knowing he would follow and Gold would be coming round the opposite way. She was, and we crossed on the far side where fewer people sat on the fountain edge. I kept walking, not looking round, but I knew what was happening twenty metres behind me. I was half expecting to hear a shot, but silencers are so good these days that even a PKK discharging a 9mm bullet just makes a soft *phutt*. I crossed the Square towards the National Gallery when I heard the result of Gold's work. Screams and shouts from the fountain area as people converged on a man who had fainted and fallen over the edge into the water. Only when they got to him and saw the hole in his head leaking blood into the fountain water and turning it crimson did they realise it was more than just a faint. I sat on the steps to the National Gallery and still couldn't see Gold.

'They won't miss him,' she said as she came from behind me and sat down. How did she do that without me seeing? She's good. 'One and a half billion others they can recruit from.'

I explained what Woodward had told me.

She was very relaxed about it; for someone who had fought Al-Qaeda and the

Taliban, I suppose the Chinese Secret Service were just run of the mill.

She laughed. 'Well, whatever is in that box must be worth a fortune. They really want it back, don't they.' It was a statement of fact, not a question; and yes, they really did want it back.

'So the job's changed. Woodward wants to know who meets with the two men that might be interested in buying some of the information inside the box, and then we get it back before it's opened – watch, retrieve and return.' That's the military name for that sort of operation.

'Not for five grand, no way.'

'Seventy-five plus expenses.'

'When do we start?' The improved amount had obviously met with approval.

'I'll fly out to Rabat later, you follow tomorrow. Get a flight to Casablanca and then a taxi to Rabat, Hotel Dar el Kabira.'

'Dar el Kabira, why that one?'

'That's where the remnants of the Madeira fracas are staying with the box. I'm going to book a room later today. I'll use the name Johnson.' Johnson was the name on one of my many fake IDs and passports.

'Dar el Kabira.' She repeated the name. 'Okay, I'll contact you there late tomorrow. Have a good trip.' And she was gone. Across the Square the area around the fountain was being taped off with crime scene tape, and the body shielded by screens as various forensic and firearm specialists from the Met were arriving. They'd better be quick, as the Chinese Embassy would be rushing to the spot to claim diplomatic immunity on the body and whisk it away as soon as the news reached them.

****

Back home at the apartment I rang my air courier company at London City Airport. They are a three-plane company, all Cessnas and good at their job. No questions asked. They had had me in and out of places where I had no right to be quite a few times.

'Rabat?' My man at the company was surprised. 'That's a new one for you, and me. Hang on.'

The line went dead for a minute before he was back. 'Got it – nearest airport is Sail, ten miles outside, how's that?'

'That's fine.'

'Small but modern, up to date Air Control, and hangars for private planes, so I'll book one. How long for?'

'Not sure, probably only be a few days, but a month to be on the safe side.'

'And I take it that when you want the return journey it will be at very short notice, and an immediate take off?'

He knows me so well. 'Yes, probably.'

'Okay, I'll take a sleeping bag and washing gear and stay with the aircraft. When do you want to go?'

'Tomorrow, about ten.'

'I'll book a take-off slot and lodge a business flight plan to Sail. Be here for nine. Usual terms apply.'

There was only ever one term.

'Cash.'

'Yes.'

I booked an Uber for 7.30am, popped out and got a KFC bucket, washed it down with French coffee whilst watching *The Irishman* for the hundredth time – I love that film – set my alarm and turned in.

****

CHAPTER 4

Sail airport was pretty quiet, and I went through Customs without any trouble and took a 'grande' taxi to Rabat and the hotel. There are two types of taxis in Morocco: big and small, or as they are known, *Grande et Petite*. The *grande* ones are usually 1990 big Mercedes and operate from city to city, or for journeys outside the cities. The *petite* ones are small Fiats and ply their trade inside the cities. Once you've been in a Moroccan city, you'll understand why. The streets are very old and very narrow, and the traffic thick and mad. Nobody takes any notice of the traffic signs and it's all out war on the roads. Never, never hire a car there, the repair bill for the bumps and scratches you will inevitably suffer will be more than your holiday cost! Imagine driving an articulated HGV through Delhi in the rush hour, multiply that by ten, and you get some idea of Moroccan traffic chaos.

I'd booked a double room on the third floor of the Dar el Kabira for seven days, a typical tourist on holiday time frame; I thought we'd have the answers we wanted by then and leave. Seven hundred pounds, including breakfast – a hundred a day seemed good value, Woodward couldn't moan at that. He would. The decor was Moroccan, and genuine at that; the rooms the same: lounge, bedroom, bathroom and walk in wardrobe, high ceilings, two beds, wall hangings and a balcony giving a view of the Medina below and the beach five hundred yards away with the blue Atlantic beyond it. Ideal.

I travel light: a change of underwear and an umbrella. I know, in Morocco? Why an umbrella? I don't know, just habit.

Gold rang on the internal phone about four o'clock. 'I'm here, I hired a silver Range Rover which is on the front concourse parking area. I'm room 23, second floor, booked in as Silver.'

'Miss or Mrs?'

'Miss.'

'Sounds better than Gold.'

'Bollocks. I see you have a suite, *Mr Johnson*. What's happening?'

'Nothing yet, we need to find out which room our friends are in.'

'Sit and watch then. I'll go down now until five when you can take over. Hourly shifts.'

'Okay.'

Sit and watch is ninety percent of what a private investigator does. You notice I say *private investigator* and not *private eye. Private* Eye is for fiction books; nobody calls us that these days.

At five o'clock I sauntered down to the lounge, took a Daily Telegraph from the papers displayed for the residents, ordered a coffee and sat beside a large palm, taking a good breeze through the open French doors that led to the patio and gardens. I had a clear view of the reception desk and entrance. I took the photo of our two marks that Woodward had given me from my inside jacket pocket and refreshed my memory, before putting it back and getting stuck into the Telegraph's right wing garbage and homage to Boris. Why doesn't he get a decent haircut? A crew cut would look better than that dishevelled haystack perched on his head.

The hotel wasn't very busy, just resident holidaymakers returning from their Medina Tour or the beach. The hour dragged; I'm not the kind of person that can sit around doing nothing – not for an hour, anyway. I did the Telegraph crossword, the small one. I got one word that fitted *four across*, but my *two down* that should have crossed it didn't fit. *Bollocks* did, so I put that in and gave up. My mobile rang; it was Gold.

'Anything?'

'No.'

'Okay, I'm on my way down.'

And that was it, the evening spent swapping places every hour with no sight of the prey. The hotel bar and lounge got busier as the evening wore on, which was good as nobody would notice our continual presence. At midnight I called a halt and we went to our respective rooms.

If you've never had a Moroccan breakfast, you are missing a real treat – dark olives with olive bread and Jben cheese, plus Moroccan spiced eggs and honey. Sounds simple, tastes wonderful.

The hotel was pretty full, so the breakfast room was busy, and Gold sat a few tables away from me. This is where we should catch first sight of our men. The breakfast was only served between seven and nine in the morning, so I took the first sitting and rang her when the waiter looked at me as though asking why I didn't bugger off as I'd had my fill and others were waiting.

I retired to the lounge with the Guardian off the resident's shelf. How they manage to fill twelve pages with nothing of interest baffles me. Journalism must be a doddle.

It was about 8.30am when our men sauntered into the room and sat down for their breakfast. I caught Gold's eye and she gave a slight nod. She had spotted them as well.

'Mr Johnson.' A voice shouted my name as I returned the paper to the rack. It was one of the reception staff, she was waving to me. I walked over, dodging between the tourists being assembled for the day's coach tour. It was the parcel from the Embassy. The reception lady handed it across the counter.

'For you, sir, arrived by courier this morning.'

'Thank you, I've been expecting it,' I said as I took it from her. 'More work.' I pulled a long face. In the large mirror behind reception I caught sight of the two men crossing from the breakfast room to the stairs with Gold behind them. It was busy, so no need for any ducking and diving; we were hidden in plain sight as the saying goes. I took the lift to my floor and suite and unpacked the guns and ammunition as I waited for Gold. A soft tap on the door and I let her in.

'My floor, room thirty-five,' she said and took one of the guns and five boxes of ammunition, filling the PKK clip with six bullets from one box before putting the gun and rest of the ammo into her shoulder bag, leaving me the other gun and five boxes. 'That's better,' she smiled and sat on one of the beds. 'I feel much better now.'

'That's the breakfast,' I said.

'No, it's the gun. Room thirty-five – handy, eh?'

I took one of Gilbert's walnuts from my bag and gave it to her. 'High up on the wall opposite their door, if you please.'

'Okay.' She took it and left the suite.

I swiped my mobile down to App Store and clicked on the walnut image. Blank screen. I sat on the bed and waited. It was only ten minutes but seemed like an age before a picture of the door to room 35 emerged on the screen as clear as could be. A hand appeared and gave the V sign. Not the V for Victory one, the other one.

Thank you, Gold. A couple of minutes later my mobile rang. It was her.

'Get it okay?'

'Yes, clear as daylight, well done. I was getting worried.'

'Had to wait for all the residents to bugger off – couldn't risk anyone seeing me and asking why I was sticking half a walnut on the wall.'

****

The rest of that day was one of the most boring I can remember. The life of a private investigator isn't one of non-stop excitement and rescuing big boobed damsels in distress from arch-villains. We spent the day in my hotel suite taking photos of anybody entering Room 35 and posting them off to Woodward on his mobile. Back would come a text: 'No Interest, Chinese Military', 'Interesting, Russian KGB', 'That's a surprise, North Korea, they couldn't afford it'. There were three other visitors of the 'no idea' variety. Gold and I took an hour out each to wander down and have a meal. At eight o'clock she'd had enough.

'I'm off to the gym for a swim, and then back to my room and an early night.'

I couldn't argue with that. Nothing would happen now.

But it did.

A suited man of about forty-five came to 35's door and knocked; a brief turn outward gave the camera a good face photo. He rang a bell somewhere with me but I couldn't put a name or place to it. I sent the photo to Woodward; no doubt he would be sitting in some posh gentlemen's club in the West End, reminiscing with old Eton and Oxford pals.

Wherever he was he was back to me in a flash, on the mobile not by text.

'Is he inside now?'

'Yes why?'

'Follow him when he comes out – let me know where he goes and get photos of who he meets.'

'Do we know him?'

'Bloody right we do. Erskin Powell, Junior Minister in the Defence Ministry, responsible for oversight of GCHQ. He's supposed to be out there at the Casablanca Arms Fair pushing laser guided technology for missiles being developed by our UK manufacturers.'

'He's not in Casablanca tonight, he's in room 35 at the Dar el Kabira.'

I switched off Woodward's mobile and called Gold on mine. 'You in the pool yet?'

'No, just put my costume on. Why?

'Number 35's in the game.'

She knew exactly what I meant. 'Okay, you follow and I'll be somewhere around.'

I changed into a black sweater and trousers, Velcro strapped my long knife to my right ankle under the trouser leg and donned a pair of soft rubber lace-up boots. The PKK went into my right-hand pocket, with a full 12 clip and twenty extra bullets into my left. Gold would have the shoulder bag, our 'tool kit' with her; she is never without it. I kept an eye on the walnut picture on my mobile and made my way down to the lounge. This time it was the Sun newspaper; no choice, it was the only one left on the rack. I settled down behind the large palm that gave me a view of the lifts and stairs. Gold wandered past and out onto the front concourse and over to a silver Range Rover and got in. I followed and slipped into the passenger seat.

'Here.' She handed me a battery pack to clip onto my belt, an earpiece and a clip-on mic. She had the same and we put them on and tested; all worked. It was another half hour before the walnut showed Powell leaving room 35 with the two others. We waited, watching the hotel main door from the car in case they had a taxi coming or a car of their own. If they had, we would have to stay close in the Medina streets or we'd easily lose them. Trouble was, staying close could also give us away. We might be lucky, as far as we knew they weren't aware of our presence; Powell would not have made the contact if there was any chance of being spotted. He must think he's in the clear.

'Here we go.' Gold nodded towards the door as our party came out. They didn't stop to wait for a taxi; they were quite jovial and kept walking towards the road. Powell was carrying the box. They crossed the road, dodging between the mass of hooting traffic, static in the usual Rabat jam, and disappeared down one of the Rabat Medina narrow streets.

'I'm off,' I said as I got out.

'I'll be somewhere near,' said Gold. I knew she would be; she always was.

I hurried through the traffic and down the narrow street. It was dark; the Medina streets have very little lighting as many are the original early 20th century streets, very narrow with high buildings each side with no windows. The windows are on the back of the buildings that usually back onto an open courtyard; on the front is just a door. The streets are organised in a grid, and most buildings painted in blue and yellow; I don't know why.

I caught sight of the trio about eighty metres in front of me in the gloom. I crossed the first crossroads.

'Over the first crossing.' I spoke quietly into the clip mic.

'Got that,' Gold answered from somewhere behind me.

Quite a few local people and a few tourists were wandering around the streets, so I got nearer to my targets without drawing attention in case they popped down a side street out of my view.

'Across next crossroads.'

'Got that.'

'Next right turn.' I followed them.

'Got that.'

This street was empty; if they stopped, I was a sitting duck. There weren't any doorways to slip into out of sight, and the bazaars were closed for the night with their gates shut at the street ends.

Shit! They had stopped and there were no people between them and me. I slowed my pace as I approached. A door opened where they stood and a swathe of light from inside the building lit them up; a few words were exchanged with somebody out of view inside, and all three entered and the door closed. I walked on and noted the number on the door, in Arabic and English.

'They've gone into number eight.'

'Number eight, got it.'

Now the problem was, how do I get into number eight? I carried on to the next crossroad; the street leading off right was just the same, houses with blank facades and a door, that would be the same right round the block and back to number eight. No way in from the front other than the doors, no alleys between the houses, and no windows. I stood in the darkest part of the street twenty yards down from number eight. What if Powell was selling the box? What should I do if he comes out without it? How many others are in the house? I needed clearance from above for my next move. I called Woodward on his mobile; I wouldn't like to pay his roaming charges. The time is the same in Morocco as in the UK, so at nine thirty he should still be up. He was, and was obviously waiting for my call.

'Well, what's he doing?'

'Yes, I'm very well, thank you for asking.'

He ignored it. 'What's he doing, Nevis?'

'He's in a house in the Medina with his two mates and at least one other. He has the box with him. Problem is, I can't get eyes on him or them – no way to get in other than by knocking at the front door. If I go in that way it will blow my cover and the job's dead.' I had my clip mic open as I talked so Gold could hear what was being said.

Woodward was quiet for a few moments. 'He's got the box with him you said?'

'Yes, but I don't know how many people are inside, so if half a dozen come out and go separate ways, I won't know which has the box, if any, and which to follow. It's your choice – I can wait and hope he comes out with the box, or go in and get it.'

'What do you think?'

'Thinking is above my pay grade.'

Gold came into my earpiece. 'Visitors, two of.'

'Hold on, Woodward, we have some action., I'll come back to you.' I shut Woodward's mobile and spoke into the mic to Gold. 'Where?' I couldn't see anybody.

'Coming from the crossroad with a sack barrow, and something on it covered by a sack.'

I couldn't see them, but I could hear them as an old metal wheeled sack barrow trundled across the cobbles. I decided to act like a tourist.

I sauntered back towards the crossroads, hands in pockets, looking around as though interested – isn't that what tourists do? I pressed against a wall as they passed me, nodding their thanks; I couldn't see what was under the sack. I let them get twenty metres on me and followed, keeping close to the house walls and the dark cover they afforded me.

They stopped at number eight and must have knocked on the door as it was opened and the light from inside lit them and their barrow up. One pulled off the cover and then both started to manhandle the cylinders of oxygen, acetylene gas and the cutting torch equipment off the barrow and into the house. They were going to try and cut the box open. I clicked the button to speed dial Woodward on his mobile.

'Well?' He sounded impatient.

'Oxy-acetylene cutting equipment has just gone in.'

His reply was immediate. 'Get the box back and get out. Use any force you need to, but get it back.' And the phone went dead.

'You hear that, Gold?' I asked.

'Yes, what's the plan?'

'No plan, just in, get the box and get out – no prisoners, no witnesses, and then home.'

'Okay, I'm twenty metres away.'

I strained my eyes in the gloom behind me but couldn't see her.

'You are?'

'Wrong way, dickhead.' From her that's a term of endearment.

I turned and looked past number eight towards the next crossroads as a quick flash of torchlight came from the darkness. She'd gone round the block and got ahead. The best way to follow somebody is from in front of them. Why? Because if somebody thinks they are being followed, they'll always assume it's from behind.

I moved to the front of the door to number eight, and took a good look round to make sure nobody else was about or coming along the street. It was all clear. Gold was next to me against the wall, hidden from anybody opening the door. I screwed the silencer onto my PKK and hammered on the door. It seemed to take an age for it to open slightly; whoever was inside clearly wasn't expecting a visitor and were being careful. The light inside the house streamed through the three-inch gap between it and the frame; I couldn't see a safety chain. I didn't wait for an invite, raising my right foot and stamping it hard against the door which sent the man behind it backwards and opened wide enough for me to step quickly inside. My first bullet nearly took his head off from close range and he slumped onto the tile floor of a hall that led forward to the courtyard twenty metres away. Closed doors were down each side; one on the right opened and our Chinese man looked out, and his face panicked as he saw me coming fast towards him – I had to get there before he could close that door. I did and side barged it into him. He stayed on his feet but stumbled backwards into the room before hitting the floor with two 9mms in his body.

At the far end of a pretty big room, under a large ceiling fan turning slowly, the box was on a wooden table. Beside it, Erskin Powell stood hands in pockets whilst the Mediterranean man watched as the two welders were readying the oxy-acetylene flame. They all turned towards me as the Chinaman hit the floor. One thing in my mind was not to put a bullet into either of the cylinders; a 9mm would go into them and then the whole lot would explode and take us all out. Acetylene is very explosive. My first worry was the Mediterranean man would be the one to carry a gun, so he got the first bullet in the head, then the two welders who were backing away towards the wall with their hands up got the next two. Sorry, chaps – Woodward said no prisoners, so no prisoners it was. I made sure with a bullet into each of their heads. Condolences to the families. Erskin Powell stood rooted to the spot, his mind working on the situation. What do you do when caught with your trousers down like this? You lie. It was a good lie, too. But you'd expect that from a politician, wouldn't you?

'Oh, thank God you got here in time,' he said, pulling out an Arms Fair ID. 'They kidnapped me from my hotel. Are you SAS?'

I smiled at him. 'No, Woodward sent me.'

'MI6 Woodward?'

'That's the man, he said to give you this.' I lifted my gun and shot him in the temple.

The welding torch had fallen to the floor, still hissing out a blue flame. That didn't interest me; the box did. I picked it up – seemed intact, strange shape, it had small ridges along the sides and, as Woodward had explained, a nine digit keyboard set into the top. The *phutt, phutt* sound of a silenced PKK firing behind me had me swing round to see another Chinaman standing facing me with a large knife in his raised hand and two exit wounds in his forehead. He pitched slowly forward onto the floor, the knife scuttling away. Gold stood in the doorway, her PKK raised.

'The other rooms are clear,' she told me, walking over to Powell's body. 'Fancy meeting you out here, Erskin.'

'A client of yours?' I asked, the answer being obvious.

'Yes, and a very good one – shame really, he was in line for a top ministerial job. With the videos I've got of him, I would have had some large contributions made to my pension fund.' She gave me a smile and put a bullet into his heart. 'Just making sure.'

A hubbub of voices reached us from outside the room. People must be coming from the communal courtyard.

'Keep them away for a minute whilst I tidy up,' said Gold.

'Tidy up?' I had no idea what she meant. 'I've got the box – come on, let's go.'

'Keep them away.' It was an order. I went to the room door and carefully looked out; she was right, there was a group of people forming up at the corridor doorway from the courtyard. I stepped out and waved my gun, and they scrambled away as fast as they could. I looked back into the room and saw Gold had doused the lit torch and was unscrewing the cylinder valves; the oxygen and acetylene gas was hissing out of them. 'Come on, let's go.' She grabbed my arm and started off back up the passage to the front door. We stepped over the dead Chinaman and out into the dark street. It was still empty. We made our way quickly back through the Medina to the main road and across into the hotel car park and into the car.

'What did you do with the cylinders, open them?'

'Yes, the gases will mix in the room and the first person to light a cigarette in there will destroy all evidence of us being there, and everything else.'

'What if they're all non-smokers?' It was a flippant remark. Don't know why I said it.

'No chance, Morocco is the top place for smokers in the world. Nobody vapes, they all still smoke.'

The explosion coming from inside the Medina could be heard quite loudly from inside the car. The deep red flames that shot into the sky above it were like a giant firework.

'Told you.' She nodded towards it. 'Won't be anything left of Powell and his buddies now. We were never there.'

'Christ!' I couldn't believe the cylinders could generate such an explosion. 'That's a historic tourist attraction we've blown up.'

'It's all right, the walls are five foot thick so the explosion went straight up and through the roof – they're mainly light tiles so no great damage problem. Few new tiles and some paint and it's back to normal. Are we going to the airport now, get out quick?'

'No.' I'd thought it through already. 'If we just leave like that, any police investigating the explosion will check the hotel registers, see two foreigners who disappeared on the night of the explosion without checking out and get interested in us. No, you check out in the morning about nine and I'll check out at ten and meet here. Get the walnut off the wall in the morning – leave it on there tonight in case there are others around who come to clean the room.' I didn't mean the hotel housekeeping staff; I meant other members of whatever organisation it is that we'd just blown up some members of. 'Give me your gun, I'll box them up and get a taxi in the morning before I meet you here and drop them back to the Embassy.'

'Okay.' She passed the gun over and left the car.

I gave Woodward a call on his mobile. He answered before the first ring had finished.

I put on an Indian accent. 'Hello, sir, this is Jamil from BT, we have a new discount call plan that we think you...'

'Just give me a report, Nevis.'

'Done and dusted – box retrieved, junior minister and several others eradicated.'

'Eradicated?'

'Totally.'

'Okay, plan?'

'Flying back tomorrow.'

'Good man, call me when you are in the air.' He rung off.

That was a most peculiar request, *call me when you are in the air* – what was Woodward up to now? I left the car and went into the hotel and up to my room.

I like hotels that have large plate glass frontages; you get a reflection of things happening behind you, or if you're somebody like me you do, as I'm always looking behind me – well, wouldn't you in my position? At night the reflection is even better, and the Moroccan figure that I'd noticed in the car park taking a lot of interest in Gold going into the hotel was taking an equal amount of interest in me. I gave her a call on her mobile from my room.

'Did you notice him?' I knew she would have.

'Yes, I thought he might follow you to your room so I stayed at the back of the lounge and watched you come in. He didn't follow you in. I'm pretty sure he was one of those who came from the courtyard in the Medina.'

'Are you still in the lounge?'

'No, I'm in my room. It's at the front of the hotel so I can watch the car park from here. He's waiting for somebody, he's been on a mobile. Are you sure we don't want to get out now? We have the box.'

'Yes, probably best if we do – he obviously knows who we are and is probably telling others where we are. Meet me in the lounge.'

I packed my gear and made my way down the stairs to the lounge. Gold was already there.

It was fairly empty as most residents were now out in the car park watching the fire brigade running hoses into the Medina. The traffic was stopped and jams stretched both ways as far as the eye could see, with honking of horns by the motorists way back in the queue who couldn't see what was happening at the front and why they were being held up. I like those situations; panic and pandemonium give great cover. Our follower would be there somewhere and I wanted him to see us and follow us, so we walked out of the hotel, over to the car and drove out of the car park, taking the road where the traffic was held up going the opposite way. Some drivers had had enough and I had to drive round them as they three-point turned to go back where they had come from; I hoped our follower had seen which way we were going. After half a mile I pulled over and we left the car outside an alleyway that led God knows where, and hoped that after our follower and his mates found our car they'd be fooled into going down it on a wild goose chase looking for us. We walked a few hundred yards on and then jumped into a Grande Taxi.

'Sail Airport.'

The driver smiled; a good fare for that time of night, and light traffic too. I called my pilot on the mobile and told him to get ready and log a flight plan back to the UK and we'd be there in an hour or so.

At the airport I paid for a week's rent on a left luggage cupboard and put the parcel with the two PKKs and the remaining ammunition inside it. I'd give the key to Woodward who could send it to the Rabat Embassy in the diplomatic bag and they could collect the box.

Customs clearance was fine, with both Gold and myself getting through without any bleepers going off or body searches. Mind you, I noticed the sly looks exchanged between a couple of young Customs officer dudes as Gold walked through, and I suspect they'd have given a lot for the opportunity to body search her!

'No company this time, sir?' shouted the pilot above the engine noise as we sped down the take off runway, giving me a knowing smile. The last time he'd flown me out of a foreign country after a job we'd been pursued down the runway by various vehicles trying to shoot the tyres out and stop us.

'I can't think what you're on about,' I shouted back, remembering only too well my heart being in my mouth on that occasion. I pay way over the usual flight fees to this company, but they ask no questions, keep to time and have never let me down. In any case, Woodward foots the bill on my expenses – or, to be precise, the UK taxpayer does.

Once in the air and into international air space, I took a coffee from the machine. Gold was asleep. I called Woodward.

'You said to call you once we were in the air.'

'Where are you landing, Heathrow?'

'No, London City.'

'Change that to Staverton.'

'Where?'

'Staverton, Gloucester.'

'Hang on.' I undid the safety belt and moved along to the pilot. 'Can we divert to Staverton Airport, Gloucester?'

He shrugged. 'Yes, can do. It's an airfield, not an airport – mainly private charter stuff and helicopters. I'll call it in, give them an ETA and book a landing slot. Be there in about two hours.' You see why I use them; no ifs and buts, just done. I went back to my seat and Woodward.

'Okay, all done – be there in two hours.'

'Good, I'll have a plain MOD car and officers pick you up.'

'Where are we going?'

'Cheltenham.'

I cottoned on. 'GCHQ.'

'Yes. I'll see you there.'

Click, and he was gone.

CHAPTER 5

Gold stirred from her sleep as we landed at Staverton. Looking out of the window, she realised we weren't at London City. 'Where are we?'

'Gloucester, Woodward's sending a car to take us to GCHQ Cheltenham.'

'Interesting, not been there before.'

Nor had I, but I had used the information gleaned by GCHQ's satellite interception of Al-Qaeda and Pakistan military *fuzz* – that's emails and mobile phone material in cyberspace – to launch many SAS attacks on their Tora Bora mountain hideouts in Afghanistan after 9/11, before the Yanks blasted it to smithereens.

The blacked-out Range Rover drove out over the tarmac to the plane's door and Gold and I transferred into it. Looking back as we made our way towards the gates, I saw the Cessna taking off again. If the Chinese had managed to put things together by now, they would know we left from Sail Airport; they'd be expecting us at

London City, as that's the destination the flight log at Sail had us listed as going to. So, surprise, surprise for anybody watching at London as an empty Cessna lands.

The security at the 'doughnut', as GCHQ is known because of its shape, was thorough. We were stopped at the main gate by security staff with mirrors on sticks used to check for bombs attached to the underside of the car, then into a large hangar of official cars and vans where armed officers escorted us through a metal detection hoop; an explosives detection dog had a good sniff, and the box was taken from me and X-rayed before it was given back to me and we left the security area into the main circular corridor with doors off it. All the doors just had alphabetical and numerical numbers. We seemed to walk a long way before being ushered through door G34 into an ante-room where Woodward was waiting with another man, a Chinaman. The Chinaman was big and broad, late middle age, bristle cut hair, and his head had no neck, it just seemed to fit into his shoulders; but the one thing that stood out was an eyepatch over his left eye. I was tempted to ask if he used to run the door at the Ministry of Sound, but Woodward wouldn't appreciate such a remark so I didn't. Woodward's probably never heard of the Ministry of Sound anyway.

'Ah, welcome back, Nevis – and you, Miss Gold. This gentleman is in charge of our ground operations in the Chinese areas of influence. The box, please.' He held out his hand and, taking the box from me, passed it the Chinaman, who was obviously not going to be introduced to us by name.

He studied it. 'Yes, this is the one.' He looked at Gold and me and smiled. 'You are very lucky to be alive.' His English was impeccable public school. 'The Guoanbu has a ten million yuang bounty on this little box.' He nodded towards a door. 'Shall we?'

Woodward nodded. 'Yes'.

Through the door was what I can only describe as an open arena, a dome-shaped place half the size of a football pitch with the walls being forty foot-high plasma screens and the floor divided into twenty foot square work places, each one with three sides being banks of computers and other technical boxes that I have no idea what their purpose was. Red, green, white, blue and yellow LEDs flashed continuously on all of them. Their masters sat in the work spaces, earphones on, tapping at various keyboards.

The Chinaman led us to a far workspace where a girl who couldn't be more than early twenties sat tapping away. She removed her headphones as we entered. Nothing was said as she took the box from the Chinaman and pushed it down into an empty cavity in her metal work surface, where it fitted the ridges perfectly with an audible click. I assumed it was from there that the box had been stolen. The keypad on top lit up. She smiled at the Chinaman. 'No damage to the keypad, sir. Shall I test it?'

'Please do.'

She tapped her keyboard and row after row of numbers scrolled down.

The Chinaman turned to me. 'The code to open the box changes every twelve hours randomly. If whoever stole it had the code for that day it would be useless in a few hours, and without the precise drawer to fit the box into to connect the keypad to the inside lock, it would be useless anyway.'

The scrolling numbers stopped and five randomly in a line of fifty went bold. The girl tapped them into the box's keypad and the top swung open on a hinge. Inside was a USB which she took out and showed to the Chinaman. 'Shall I?'

'Yes please.'

She pushed it into one of many USB portals in the bank of flashing computers stacked in her workstation and tapped the five numbers into her keyboard.

The Chinaman pointed to the forty-foot plasma screen nearest to us. 'Observe.'

What we *observed* was a blue background with literally hundreds of oblong squares dotted over it in no particular order, each with a line of alphabetical and numerical codes.

'Please explain for our visitors,' the Chinaman asked the girl.

She pointed from one set of codes to another as she talked. 'Each of those codes represents one of our defence early warning satellites, most over the Chinese Republic and Russia. They give our listening posts...' She pointed towards other occupied workstations in the room, '...access to cyber and telephone conversations, as well as visual sight of military and other installations, and immediate notice of missile launches.'

'Spy satellites,' said the Chinaman, 'every major power has them. And every major power wants to knock out the opposition's, which is what this little caper has been about.'

Little caper? Well, if he thinks this has been a *little caper*, God knows what he classes as a big one!

The girl continued. 'The numbers and letters you see on each satellite site are the codes to access their operating motherboards, and in enemy hands, with the USB from that box...'

She pointed to the box, '...and a little bit of programming knowledge, an enemy could get into and either destroy the satellite's transmission or change its orbit and send it into the earth's atmosphere where it would burn up, and our defence would be compromised.'

'Hang on.' I was confused. 'So how have the satellites been operating without the USB from the box?'

Woodward smiled. 'Backup, Nevis, we have a backup one. The point being that had that USB got into enemy hands, we would have had to change every satellite code individually,'

'So why not just do that then instead of chasing the box?'

'Three months' work at least, and within that time anybody with the codes would have access to the satellites and be able to knock them out. No, that box must never fall into the wrong hands.'

'What's ten million yuang?' asked Gold.

'Roughly a million and a quarter in sterling,' said the Chinaman.

Gold looked at me. 'We've been done.'

Woodward ignored the remark. 'Right, I'll get you two a car to take you home, and you and I can meet in the morning, Nevis. Preferably not at a British Rail cafe.'

'Why do we need to meet in the morning?' I didn't see the purpose of that.

'I need to know how the box made its way out of here and who is mastermind behind it. Your job isn't finished yet.'

'Erskin Powell, and he's dead.'

Woodward laughed. 'Erskin Powell was a pawn, not a mastermind – he was used to get information because he was a junior minister, and had access to documents and restricted places.'

'Like here,' added the Chinaman. 'That box didn't walk out on its own one night, Mr Nevis. Powell recruited somebody on the staff who took it, and that somebody obviously has access to the building and is on the staff. We need to know who, and who they passed the box to.'

Woodward was impatiently checking his watch. 'I need to brief the PM – eleven o'clock in the morning at your office, Nevis, and I'll update you on what we know.'

'Eleven o'clock at the BR café, or we don't meet.' I was adamant on that. When a job is ongoing I never, but never, use the office. Obviously if somebody is out to get me that's the first place they'll stake out.

'Oh, very well, if you insist.' Woodward led the way out of the dome, not even giving a *'goodbye and thank you'* to the girl. I gave her a smile and a wave, which she returned. I'm nice like that; being polite doesn't cost anything. Sometimes I apologise to people before I kill them.

****

It's very nice to be chauffeur driven in a top of the range Mercedes Benz SUV; probably bullet-proof as well, the glass panel between the back passenger seats and the driver and co-driver looked thick enough. I could tell by the silence that Gold was thinking things through, as was I.

'I think we ought to finish this.' She spoke as we sped past the Swindon turn-off on the M4.

'Finish it? You mean back out?'

'No, no way, the opposite. Obviously whoever stole the box knows we were responsible for getting it back. The Arab chap at the hotel car park, he was watching us, so whoever his bosses are would have checked the hotel register – okay, we used false names, but hotel CCTV could show us. Don't forget the Chinaman in Trafalgar Square, they'd spotted you back then and could only have done that by getting info and descriptions from Madeira – and the only way they'd have got that was from the one chap who limped away from the toboggan wreckage. They've got our number, Ben – we need to be ahead of them and strike first.'

She was making sense, she always did.

****

CHAPTER 6

Surprise, surprise! Eleven o'clock at Charing Cross Station Concourse cafe and I was joined at my window table by Woodward, who made a great show again of flipping non-existent crumbs off his seat with his leather gloves before sitting down; and this time he had brought with him the Chinaman. Gold would be watching from somewhere and would be as surprised as me. Woodward was carrying a manila folder. As usual the two protection officers accompanying them sat a few tables behind against the rear wall, which gave them a clear view of everything in front and not having to worry about anything behind. Training, you never forget it. Woodward and the Chinaman unbuttoned their overcoats in unison and shifted their seats into the table.

They both declined my offer of coffees. The Chinaman had obviously been made aware of the potential health issues of British Rail coffee.

'We haven't been introduced.' I looked from Woodward to the Chinaman.

Nothing; we obviously weren't going to be introduced. Woodward opened the folder and took out some 10 x 8 black and white photos. I guessed they'd been taken by surveillance officers. I was right. He passed the first one over to me. It was of the main entrance to the Chinese MMS building in Shizhao, a city west of Beijing. The building is a very large seven-storey modern block with a massive cathedral-like entrance. The photo showed Erskin Powell with a Chinese man walking into the building. The second photo Woodward passed across showed Powell leaving alone.

'That building is China's equivalent to GCHQ,' explained the Chinaman.

'Those were taken when Powell was supposed to be on holiday in Madeira,' added Woodward. 'His favourite holiday destination – he has an apartment there.

'He *had* an apartment there,' I corrected him.

'Yes, had an apartment there,' he agreed. 'It was cleaned early this morning by a removal company – everything taken out to the island's waste incinerator and burnt, and then the place sprayed with bleach.'

'Which destroys fingerprints and DNA.'

'Exactly. Whoever had been in that apartment with Powell didn't want any trace left. And we believe these are the people who would have been there at some time.' He passed three more photos across to me. The first one was of two Moroccans walking through the Madeira Airport Arrivals green zone Customs area. 'Their names aren't important – both are from the Moroccan Secret Service, the DST, Direction de la Surveillance du Territoire. We suspect that they were the two at the viewing platform who chased you onto the toboggans. The one on the left we believe was killed in the fall as he hasn't been seen since, whilst the one on the right is the man with the limp, caused by the fall. He survived with the box.'

'Yes, I recognise him from the photos you showed me of the freighter docked at Rabat – he was coming off it with the other Oriental chap. He had the box.'

'Correct.'

The second photo showed Erskin Powell at the Casablanca Arms Fair, seated at a large UK trade stand with four other people. All Chinese.

The Chinaman explained. 'All four are from the Chinese MSS – two are secret service acting as protection, the other two are known to be weapons analysts. We believe this is the meeting where Powell confirmed that the box had successfully been stolen from GCHQ, and they had probably been shown pictures of it to confirm it was the right box at some time before this meeting.'

Woodward took over. 'The pictures you sent me of the people visiting the hotel room where the box was confirmed that a deal was going through. The clincher was when Powell visited – at that point it was thought that the box would disappear with the Chinese, and that would mean that all those satellite codes you saw yesterday at GCHQ would have to be cancelled, leaving our umbrella missile defence system down and the country very vulnerable until we replaced them. We had to act then and retrieve the box.'

'That's all done now and we thank you and your partner,' said the Chinaman with a smile. He used the term '*we*', so he was MI6.

'Now,' Woodward said. 'We need to eliminate the others. Third photo.'

The third photo showed the inside of a large, high class Chinese restaurant. Powell sat at a table, obviously enjoying a meal with four others: three Chinese and one late middle-aged Englishman.

'Taken by one of our undercover men at the Lotus Flower Restaurant, Gerrard Street. You may recognise one of the Chinese gentlemen as the one who got assassinated by *person unknown* in Trafalgar Square.' The look Woodward gave me told me he knew exactly who *person unknown* was. 'Then there's Powell, two other Chinese, and one Englishman.'

The Chinaman interrupted. 'The two Chinese, and the one killed by *person unknown*, are from the Chinese Embassy, listed as cultural attaches but in reality MSS. This photo and a strongly worded letter have been sent to the Chinese Ambassador this morning asking for information on who they are and what part they play in the death abroad of one of HM's Government ministers. It's all bluff and counter bluff – the Chinese know we are involved as much as we know they are involved, but the outcome will be that the two MSS men will be returned to China. They are of no use over here now as we plainly know who they are.'

That was a slight relief to me; two less to deal with. That only leaves one billion, five hundred thousand, nine hundred and ninety-seven left to deal with.

'But the Englishman won't be going anywhere,' added Woodward. 'He is Desmond River, property developer, industrialist, arms dealer and media baron – fingers in many pies, most of them verging on the illegal. Given a CBE in the last PM's honours list for services to charity. Like most of the dodgy rich in the UK, you swindle your way to immense fortune and then gain an air of legitimacy with a big donation to charity or the Tory party. He did both, plus a sizeable contribution to Erskin Powell's election campaign fund.' Woodward looked me straight in the eye. 'A nasty piece of work, Nevis – be of no doubt that to tangle with River is a walk on the real wild side. No quarter given. He'd have you killed without a second thought.'

'So why hasn't he?'

'Because he doesn't know who you are. He no doubt has a picture of you and Miss Gold taken in Rabat and a description, but no names. He would have worked out that you are either MI6 or maybe N14 seconded to MI6. But most of all he knows you buggered up his big pay day and took the box back.'

'Not my biggest fan then,' I remarked.

'Indeed not.' Woodward smiled.

'Okay, so thanks for the heads-up.' I had already worked out that I had to get to this Desmond River and kill him before he or his men got to me. He didn't seem the kind of man who allowed others to cock up his plans and get away without retribution.

Woodward was serious. 'It's not a heads-up, Nevis, it's a job. He's your mark. Find out how he got the box out of GCHQ and then eliminate him. He obviously has somebody inside there on his payroll, or on a blackmail list. Find out who first.'

I took a deep breath. 'One thing that bothers me, Mr Woodward – at the beginning of all this you hired me to follow a man carrying the box. He went to Madeira and was thrown off a viewpoint for the box. Who was he?'

'Erskin Powell's brother.'

'Who worked at GCHQ?' It seemed an obvious assumption.

'No, he was a tailor.'

'A tailor? So how did he get involved?'

'Probably for money. His business accounts show it was near to bankruptcy for the last year, so we assume Erskin offered him a good amount of money to take the box to his Madeira apartment, and then he was told to meet the Chinese pair at the viewpoint.'

'Okay.' Seemed a reasonable explanation. 'So why did the Chinese take the box from Madeira to Rabat? Why not Beijing or Shizhao?

The Chinaman answered. 'To take it direct to China would have given us proof that they, the Chinese, were directly involved in its theft and would create a diplomatic incident. A Chinese theft of a NATO country's military secrets would have had all of NATO howling furiously, and probably raising trade sanctions on Chinese imports. One thing China fears are trade sanctions that could cripple its economy in months. China is pouring money and resources into Morocco and the surrounding Western North African countries – Algeria, Mali, Mauritania, and others who all have mineral wealth but not the money or expertise to mine and sell it. China has that money and expertise, and is already well entrenched in that area. They have an Embassy in Rabat, and that was the nearest place that the box could have been offloaded and into a diplomatic bag and onto the MSS HQ in Shizhoa.'

'Bloody hell, Mr Woodward.' I shook my head. 'You put me into what you described in the beginning as a surveillance job, and now I've destroyed Madeira's tourist industry, blown up buildings in a foreign country, killed Chinese secret agents, killed one of Her Majesty's Ministers, and now I'm targeting a big noise in British business who has a CBE.'

Woodward knew me so well. 'All right, Nevis, an extra twenty-five on top.'

When you break it down, it's not a great amount for this kind of specialist work, is it? A hundred grand a week split between Gold and me is fifty grand each for seven days' work, which is just over seven grand a day for putting our lives on the line. But you gotta eat, haven't you, eh?

'Okay,' I said. 'And a CBE.'

They both laughed. 'Okay,' Woodward nodded. 'I'll have a word with the PM when it's all over.'

'By then it'll probably be a posthumous one.'

'Right.' Woodward rose to go, followed by the Chinaman. 'Two objectives then Nevis – how did they get the box out, and then put an end to Desmond River. Stay in touch, dear boy.'

And off they went.

****

CHAPTER 7

My office is what estate agents call *'bespoke'* when they can't think of anything good to say about a property: two rooms, a small kitchen and a toilet.

'So what's the plan?' Gold had her feet up on my office desk, chomping through a doner kebab from the Kurzine Restaurant and Takeaway which is very handily placed just down the Borough High Street from the office, and run by the owner Memet. I did a favour for Memet a couple of years ago when his daughter was getting too far in with a nasty piece of work, and ever since he won't let me pay for anything; so I usually order and put a tenner on the counter and run off with the kebab before he can stop me.

I chewed and swallowed the last piece of goat testicle or whatever other offal goes into a doner kebab. That's the thing about takeaway foods; whatever you do, don't think about what is actually in them, just enjoy the taste. I went to the kitchen and washed and dried my hands.

'The plan,' I said. 'Is to get inside River's business and stir things up. He's obviously the money man and is pulling the strings.'

'Do you think they'll have another go at getting the box?'

I shrugged. 'Depends on what the Chinese say. If they've paid a lot of dosh to River for it, they won't be happy with nothing for their money. He'd be sensible to give it back or have another go at lifting the box from GCHQ. From what Woodward said, I don't think he'll let it go.''

'Right.' Gold went to the kitchen and washed and dried her hands. 'First thing is to find out what we can about Desmond River.' She clicked on the desk computer. 'He sounds like a reggae artist from the sixties.'

'That was Desmond *Dekker*.'

If looks could kill. 'I know that, I was just saying.'

Then came the put-down. 'Do something useful – hoover your office, it's thick with dust.'

****

I didn't hoover the office straight away, but I sorted through Gold's shoulder bag and took out one of the walnuts; it had occurred to me it could be useful in the office. I stuck it above the door facing inside the office, switched it on and opened the app on my mobile. Perfect! I had a good view of the office and the kitchen and toilet doors. If anybody came in when I wasn't there, I'd have them on screen. Then, as Gold was still on the computer, I did hoover the office, ignoring her nasty looks when I bumped her chair leg, the desk legs or her feet. All accidental, of course. Two hours and two coffees later, Gold hit the print button and sat back as the results of her work clicked out of the printer. Three printed pages and three copy photos.

'Done?' I asked and pulled up a chair next to her.

'Interesting man is Desmond River.' She stapled the pages together and passed them to me. 'Read.'

I read. Interesting man indeed. Real name Striglov; parents Russian. Father took advantage of Yeltsin's debacle and became owner of a major utilities company supplying gas and electricity. Fell out with Putin and fled to the UK, where he changed the family name by deed poll to River; made sure his money, a few billion in sterling taken from the utility company, had fled before him. Extradition back to Russia requested and refused. Died with his wife in a car crash labelled suspicious by the investigating police. Only child Desmond was by this time running the family businesses and had invested in early satellite technology, partnering Chinese company Huawei as they made inroads into western communication systems including 4G, 5G and satellite. Married to a Chinese lady, Sun Zalny, in Beijing twelve years ago; she is the daughter of a prominent member of the standing committee of the Politburo. Their main residence is a gated mansion in the Cotswolds, handy for Cheltenham and GCHQ, and they have a town house in South Eaton Place, Belgravia. No children. River gives financial donations to all political parties and many individual MPs who lobby on his behalf when asked, including Erskin Powell. River has been named by the CIA as a 'person of interest' and refused entry to the USA. He was nominated for a board position on the CBI, but some dodgy election practices involving bribes were discovered and scuppered that little enterprise; his membership was terminated. The three photos were a recent one of him at a white tie event with his wife, his business HQ building at Canary Wharf where he rents a floor, and one of his Cotswold mansions, or what you can see of it behind tall iron gates, razor wire on the top of the high surround walls and CCTV cameras in profusion. Desmond River is keen on his privacy.

I rubbed my eyes; this was a hard one. I looked at Gold, who was checking her phone messages. 'It's a blank canvas, no suspects inside GCHQ. Where do we start?'

'Surveillance.'

'Of?'

'River. If he's going to try for that box again, he's going to have to put a plan together that will have to involve a GCHQ staff member. We just have to find out which one, and the only way we will do that is to see if he meets somebody who works there.'

'He might not meet them face to face, he might phone or email on the dark web. He's not stupid, is he?'

'He was stupid enough to meet that lot in a public restaurant.' Gold finger-stabbed the restaurant photo, 'Maybe we should start there, stir things up. They, whoever *they* are, know you're involved, so what better way to open up the can of worms than for you to visit the restaurant and start asking questions? Chinatown is a very tight community, and word of your visit will soon get around.'

****

CHAPTER 8

The Lotus Flower Chinese restaurant in Gerrard Street was quite busy. It was lunchtime the next day, and we had a plan.

I showed the staff at the door the photo and asked if they knew who the people in it were. They spoke to each other in Chinese, and then told me to wait whilst one scuttled away and returned with an older man, maybe the manager; he was treated with deference by the staff who bowed as he approached.

'Can I help you, sir?' The smile was false, the English perfect.

I took my false police ID from my pocket and showed it to him. It's a good one; DCS Dick Clancy of the Organised Crime Squad had it made up for me for use in a sting I did for him some time ago, and somehow I had forgotten to give it back. I gave the man the photo.

'We are trying to trace these men. They ate in your restaurant recently. Can you put any names to the faces?'

He took his time looking at the photo. He shook his head. 'No, I don't know any of them – just ordinary customers, not regulars.' He waved a hand at the crowded tables. 'As you can see, we are a very busy restaurant.'

I had done what I wanted to do, thanked him and left, hurrying back to my car in Chinatown Masterpark at Newport Place. I called Gold.

'All done, the manager knew the faces but said he didn't. I'm going back to watch.'

'Okay. If River leaves his office I'll call you.'

Gold was parked up watching River's office. If the plan worked, my visit to the Lotus Flower would create enough panic to bring things out into the open and move them along. I took a tin from the glove compartment and selected a fake moustache from the three inside, took a blob of adhesive from a tube and, using the rear mirror, put it in place before adding a pair of plain glasses and a beret to my disguise. I took a lightweight fawn Macintosh from the rear seat, leaving the dark blue jacket that I had worn inside the restaurant in its place; and happy that I didn't look anything like the man who had been asking questions, I made my way back to Gerrard Street and a window seat in a coffee bar that gave me a good view of the Lotus Flower. I paid for a prawn and mayonnaise sandwich and a coffee and settled down.

It took about twenty minutes and a second cup of coffee before they arrived: two Chinese gentlemen dropped off by a car with diplomatic plates that waited outside. I guessed they'd be either showing the manager a photo of me or taking a look at the restaurant's CCTV to identify me. So now we knew the Lotus Flower, or at least the manager, was involved. I let Gold know.

'Bingo, diplomatic car and occupants arrived.'

'No movement here.'

I was already on my way back to my car, and I left the car park and pulled in fifty metres behind the diplomatic car and waited. It was another ten minutes before they emerged with the manager, and after a conversation at the kerbside and some bows they got into the car and drove off. I followed. I reckoned there were four choices of destination: the Chinese embassy, River's office, River's Cotswolds home, or Cheltenham.

It was River's office. I pulled up behind Gold's car at Canary Wharf and she got out and joined me in mine. I noticed she had the shoulder bag with her, just in case.

'Moustache suits you.'

I had forgotten it was still stuck on. I pulled it off gently as we watched the two Chinese gents leave their car and hurry up the wide steps into River's office building.

'Follow?' asked Gold.

'No point, we wouldn't be able to get inside and listen. They're obviously going to let him know I'm asking questions, so hopefully that'll create a little concern.'

It did. Fifteen minutes later, the Chinese came out together with River. They waited until his chauffeured car arrived and all got in. The diplomatic car left the wharf behind them and took a different route.

'He's off back to the Embassy,' Gold said. 'I wonder where River is going?'

My office, that's where River was going. We followed at a distance, and when they parked up a few spaces past the office entrance I swung off the road into the underground car park and into one of my two spaces. Gold fished the shoulder bag off the back seat and we geared up with earpiece, clip-on mic and battery pack. I took a PKK and slotted in a full clip and screwed on a silencer before leaving the car. At the stairwell I tested the mic.

'One, two, three, testing.'

'Loud and clear, I'm taking a walk to the street,' said Gold.

I flicked on my mobile as I climbed the stairs and activated the walnut app. The office was empty. I needed to know where the two goons were; had they left River's car? I didn't want to come face to face with them on the stairs or in the corridor.

'The two have left the car and are inside your building,' Gold updated me.

'Copy.'

I could hear the lift; they must have waited on the ground floor and taken it up. I wished the walnut had sound, as I'd be able to hear if they knocked at the office door.

They didn't knock. All I saw on the mobile's screen was my office door opening slowly into the office; they must have lock picks, or they had busted it open. Both men entered below the camera, guns held in front. They did a quick look around, checked the kitchen and toilet, and then stood having a conversation. By now I was on my floor at the end of the corridor by the lift. It took me a couple of seconds to figure out what they were doing next. They were going to lie in wait for me, hiding in the office. Number one goon went into the toilet and shut the door, leaving a small gap to look through. Number two shut the office door, so they must have picked the lock, and then he went out of view as he flattened himself against the wall beside it, so that he would be hidden to anybody opening the door. He obviously wasn't aware that cheapskate London landlords use plasterboard walling to cut costs. I moved quietly along the corridor, keeping an eye on the App until I was outside beside the door, right on the other side of the plasterboard to the goon. I flicked the phone shut and put it in my pocket. I put a 9mm bullet through the wall into goon number one as I kicked open the door, and stepping into the office sent bullet number two through the toilet door, as did number three after it before I turned and put number four in the head of goon one who had slumped to the floor with an exit wound above his heart. A grunt from the toilet said number two needed my attention. I put two more bullets through the door knee-high, as I assumed he'd be down on them by now. I moved to the side of the toilet in case he was still able to fire back through the door and slid a new clip of six into the PKK. I gave it two minutes and heard nothing from the toilet before slowly pushing open the door from the side. I expected it to hit against a body, but it didn't. It didn't because goon two was leant over the toilet like a man in prayer. Only men in prayer don't usually have blood seeping through the back of their jacket and a bullet hole in the back of their neck. He was dead too.

I clicked on my mic. 'All done, all clear up here.'

'Much of a mess?' Gold asked.

'Pretty much, need to get the cleaners in and pay a visit to the magician's.'

'Okay.'

'What's happening outside?'

'River is sitting in his car. Looks like he's waiting for them to return.'

'He'll have a long wait. I'll come down and wander out as though I'm looking for somebody. That should tell him his goons failed and he should drive off then.'

'Okay. I'll be opposite as near to his car as I can get, in case he gets any ideas of taking a shot himself.'

'Nah, he won't do that. He'll run. I want to put a tracker on his car - meet me in the garage first.'

I went into the kitchen and reached into the cupboard under the sink and behind a row of toilet rolls where I keep my trackers; useful little tools are trackers, means you don't have to follow a car. Mine are from Gilbert's, all programmed to send a signal to another of his homemade apps that tell you which direction to go to find it. I took one out, tested the battery was fine – it was – and shutting and locking the office door behind me, hurried down to Gold who was already waiting at the back of the garage.

'Bumper magnetic?' she asked.

'Yes, but put it in the wheel arch – less vibration, less chance of it being shaken off.'

'Okay.'

She went back up the ramp to the street and I took the stairs to the ground floor. I gave her a couple of minutes to get into position before holding my hand inside my jacket, as though I might just have a gun in a shoulder holster. I didn't have one; I'd purposely left it in the office. Gold would cover me. One thing constant on every job I did was *'Gold would cover me'*.

I walked outside, making it obvious I was looking for something or someone. I could see River's car; you couldn't miss a Bentley in the Borough High Street. He would have seen me and not seen Gold bob down and push the tracker up under the rear wheel arch. He was expecting the goons; he was expecting me to be dead. The Bentley moved from the kerb and away up the street. I didn't give it a second glance. Where was he going now?

Gold came over. 'Pity we haven't got ANPR access.'

My mind raced; we could have. I needed to make a call. 'Come on, got a couple of calls to make.'

Back in the office Gold surveyed the scene. 'Once River reports to his Chinese handler they'll come looking.'

'Yes, I know.' I scrolled down my contacts list on the mobile and speed dialled '*Magicians*'.

The couple of old-time crooks known as the 'magicians' ran a crematorium in south London – well, they didn't actually run it, the council did; they were employed there and did the actual cremating in the cellar beneath the public bit. When father's coffin lowered out of view from the public bit, the magicians lit the gas and did the rest. They also did a bit of freelance work at night for people who needed to make a body disappear a bit sharpish, hence their nickname '*the magicians*'. I don't even know their real names – not that I want to, and certainly not what they would want either. I first met them eight years ago after sorting out a gang feud for a client that left six bodies in an East End warehouse. That time they did a 'cash and collect' service, but even then they looked old; now I reckon they are in their eighties. I've used them a few times myself since then and never had a problem.

The number rang twice before a gruff voice answered.

'Yes?'

'Ben Nevis.'

'I know, you're on my mobile's contact list. What can we do for you?'

'A party of two, urgent.'

'Never simple with you Ben, is it? Can't you just do singles?'

'Can't help it when they come at me in pairs.'

'We don't do call and collect anymore, Ben – getting too old, slowing down, arthritic knees. You'll have to bring the party here. How does ten o'clock suit?'

'I'll be there.'

'Back gate at ten then, and Ben...'

'I know, cash only.'

'Two grand.'

'Blimey, that's gone up – it was five hundred each last time.'

'Fuel costs, Ben, price of gas has hit the roof – blame the Russians. Ten o'clock, don't be late.'

And the phone clicked off. My next call was to the cleaners. Many silly crooks wouldn't be behind prison bars if they had used cleaners after a job. My cleaners are a husband-and-wife team. They would come in and totally deep clean the place top to tail; all the blood stains would be gone, no fibres of clothing, no hairs, no fingerprints, all gone and the whole place sprayed with bleach which disintegrates DNA and any fingerprints the cleaners may miss. My cleaners are a real commercial cleaning company who move into business offices overnight and clear the previous day's rubbish, leaving them spick and span for the next morning. Hence their name.

'Spick and Span Cleaners. Mr Nevis, what can we do for you?'

Somebody else who had my mobile on their contact list.

'I need a deep clean.'

'The office?'

'Yes.'

'How deep a clean? Blood?'

'Quite a lot of it, yes.'

'When?'

'As soon as possible.'

'An hour?'

'That's fine, and an internal door needs replacing.'

'Okay, five hundred – cash.'

You see how expensive it is to kill somebody. 'Okay, I'll leave it and the key with Memet in the kebab shop along the road.'

'Okay.'

Spick and Span rang off. We had an hour to get the two bodies out before they arrived. And, no, I haven't got rugs to roll them up in – this is real, not a Netflix narco series. The whole office is lino or whatever it's called these days, easy to clean blood off of. I'd removed a body from the office before, so had a plan. I left Gold to hold the fort and went along the High Street to the builder merchants and bought four large thick plastic garden waste bags. Back in the office, we slipped one over the head of each goon and the other ones up over the feet. Where the bags over lapped we gaffer taped them together. I had a few reels of that in the kitchen cupboard; handy for so many things is gaffer tape, never be without it.

I was quite pleased to get the two bodies securely inside a plastic bag, as sometimes a corpse will open its orifices – not pleasant. We carried them to the lift, I locked the office door, and together we put them in the lift and took them to the lower-ground garage floor and into the boot of my Range Rover, where I pulled the security blind from the rear seats over them. I left Gold in the garage and went along the road to the bank and took out two grand. I always carry a grand in a small money belt round my left ankle, so I had enough to pay the cleaners and the magicians. I went into the kebab house and gave Memet the cleaners' money and the keys. Back in the garage we checked the tracker app. River was still moving, and moving west outside London.

'Homeward bound, the Cotswolds?' suggested Gold.

'Yes, more than likely,' I agreed. 'I'll get Clancy to check it out on ANPR later. First, we need to get you back to your motor at Canary Wharf before it's towed away. Then I'm going home for a snooze and something to eat before I visit the magicians.'

****

The digital clock on the dash showed 10.00pm. I was parked a hundred metres up the road from the back entrance to the crematorium. I called the magicians on the mobile.

'You outside, Ben?'

'Yes.'

'Okay, come on in.'

I drove up to the tall steel back gates and they automatically opened inwards. Once inside I followed the narrow tarmac road through some trees to the side of the building. A door was already open, and the magicians stood beside it in blue plastic overalls with a hospital patient trolly. They reminded me of characters in a UK TV programme called 'Last of the Summer Wine'; *Foggy* and *Clegg* would fit a description of the magicians perfectly. I pulled up and got out; no words of welcome or asking about my health, the trolley was pushed to the rear of the Range Rover, boot opened, security screen lifted, and between them they lifted out the body bags, accompanied by a lot of grunting and puffing, put them on the trolley and wheeled it back inside the building. *Foggy* came back out and gave me a smile as I already had their money in my hand. He took it, which broadened his smile further.

'Thank you, Ben, always a pleasure to do business with you. How's Miss Gold?'

'She sends her best wishes.' She hadn't, but it sounded good. Last time Gold had come there with me, *Foggy* had goosed her as she got back into the car. Anybody else and they'd have been laid out with one punch, but Gold knew the value of the magicians to us and had just smiled and called him a 'naughty boy'. He'd liked that, silly old fart. I got back in the car. 'Until the next time then.'

He waved a hand, turned and went through the door, shutting it behind him. I drove slowly to the gate which was swinging back open. Once out onto the road, I parked up again a hundred metres along the road, waited and watched. It took twenty minutes, and then the tall crematorium chimney began to smoke. Job done. I drove home; it had been one hell of a day, sleep was needed.

****

CHAPTER 9

I rang Gold in the morning and told her what I was going to do and that I'd ring her when I found out where Desmond River was. The app was flashing South West of London, so I thought that must be his place in the Cotswolds

I gave Dick Clancy a ring. Clancy is top honcho in the Met's Organised Crime Squad and was my boss for the ten years I spent there after I left MI6. Since I went private, he has put quite a lot of work my way; mainly surveillance, but a few hits that had to be made *off piste* as the saying in the Squad goes – in other words, by somebody that can't be connected back to them; somebody like me who will pull the trigger for money and ask no questions. Well, that's not entirely true, because if MI6 gives me a hit to make I know the mark isn't exactly going to be a nice person, is he, or she? If I have a conscience, it's clear.

Clancy was okay with my request, and an hour later I hip swerved through the concrete security blocks outside West End Central police station in Harley Street and checked in at the desk who had my name down on the visitors' list, and made my way up to Clancy's office.

'You're a pain in the butt, Nevis.'

I've had worse greetings

'Good morning, Mr Clancy, how nice to see you too,' I countered.

He waved me to sit down opposite him at the desk and pushed a stapled trio of printed papers over to me. 'That's the route of the car you wanted.'

It was a printout of the route River had taken the day before. Clancy had got the car's registration number fed into the ANPR system and had a printout generated from it. It confirmed my suspicion from the app; River had finished up at his Cotswold home, and the app showed he was still there.'

Clancy leaned back in his chair and put his hands behind his head. He always did that when it was question time. It was.

'So why are you interested in Desmond River?'

He'd done his homework with the DVLA on the car's owner.

'State secret, can't say.'

He nodded. 'Okay, then in that case your car and Gold's car will be clamped whenever and wherever they are parked until I get an answer.' He gave me a 'got you' smile. 'I don't suppose Miss Gold would appreciate that?'

No, she definitely would not. I knew anything I told Clancy would remain between us, as I knew things about his department's past operations that he wouldn't want put in the public domain; and he certainly knew things about me that would lift me out of the public domain and into Her Majesty's prison domain.

'He's involved in trading defence satellite secrets with China.'

'Wow!' That shocked Clancy. 'That is a surprise. He's on our *persons of interest* list, but nothing that serious – mainly for the company he keeps, dodgy financiers and hedge fund people. Moves a lot of money around through his various businesses when there's no need, which is a sure sign of money laundering. He doesn't pay a penny in tax, got all his businesses registered in Panama. The financial forensic boys have their eye on him too. He is one of those bastards who we know is bad to the core but can't nail. If he should have an accident, a fatal one, we wouldn't be inclined to investigate, even if it was suspicious.'

Enough said, eh? If that wasn't a hint, nothing was.

'Can we check where the car is now? I think it's still at the same place, but wouldn't mind a quick check,' I asked.

'Follow.' Clancy stood, came round from his desk and we went into the main OC Team Room where a few officers, most looking like dodgy characters and others as smart city slickers, worked away at desks and screens. Clancy led me to the far end wall and a very large plasma screen lit up with a map of the streets of London. He held out his hand for the printout and on a keyboard tapped in the car's registration number. It took a few seconds for the screen to scroll down and sideways left and then settle on a place called Whittington off the A40 outside Cheltenham. 'Got a pen?' Clancy asked.

I picked up a biro from the nearest desk and passed it to him, and he wrote something on the printout.

'Postcode of where the car is now, so I would assume that's River's house postcode too.' He handed the printout back to me. 'All yours, Ben – have fun, and do keep it out of the papers.'

I left Clancy and sat in my car for a while, thinking about the next move. If anybody was about to give me grief, like some pissed off Chinese Embassy goons, I needed to lose them before going for River. I gave Gold a call.

'I'm busy.'

'Put down the whip, take off the thigh boots, apologise to the client, but your mother's been rushed to hospital.'

'That's a good one, I'll try that. What's the plan?'

'I'm going back to the office to see if anything's in play.'

'Okay, I'll be there in forty minutes.'

She rang off. Alyson Gold, ex Mossad, ex Flotilla 13, had developed a scheme in her youth of tempting elderly rich gentlemen with all sorts of sexual shenanigans except the actual act. The promise of the final consummation kept the stupid old codgers on the hook, parting with more and more money, until she thought she'd got as much as she could and then dropped them like a hot coal. None ever sued or chased her through the courts for reimbursement, as she always made sure videos were made of their antics. Not the sort of videos their wives, business associates or fellow MPs were likely to enjoy watching. Well, maybe the MPs would. After a commended stint in the military with

Mossad and a chance meeting with me when we both provided back up for the US forces that eliminated Bin Laden in Pakistan, we lost contact for a few years and then renewed it when too many members of the Israeli Knesset compared notes on their reasons for resigning and one name kept coming up: Alyson Gold, known to Lahav 433 – the Israeli police corruption unit – as the Gold Digger, and she quickly disappeared as the net closed, to surface in London a year later and start *gold digging* here. Unfortunately for her, one of her marks was a good client of mine and I sussed out her game pretty quickly and the reunion happened, which resulted in her joining me as a back-up and also continuing her own 'work'.

I gave her forty-five minutes before parking in a back street, taking my PKK and shoulder holster from the glove compartment and slipping them on before sauntering along the Borough High Street to my office building. If anybody was coming for me, I wanted to hold out an open invitation – all comers welcome, bring your own body bag. I didn't have radio contact with Gold, but I knew she'd be there somewhere in the background watching my back. I walked down into the basement car park. Nobody followed. I hit the first and second floor buttons in the lift and got out before the doors closed and raced up the stairs, getting to my second floor before it did. I pulled out my gun and slipped the safety catch off, then kneeling low on the stairs peeped round at floor level. The lift shaft was this stairwell end of the corridor.

He was waiting; another Chinaman, just the one this time – didn't I warrant two anymore? He had his gun in the standard two-handed, knees bent position aimed at the lift, obviously expecting the doors to open and reveal his target: me. The lift reached the floor and pinged as the doors opened. I hit him in the side of his head before they opened wide enough to show empty. The 9mm went through and I'd have to find it later; they're pretty big. I could have used a .22 clip but they tend to stick inside the skull, not enough power to push through two lots of bone. The .22 could kill but also might just bounce about the brain, leaving the victim alive but brain dead – not nice. A clean kill is always preferable. Plus with two holes in the head, the blood won't spurt out and tends to dribble or stay inside. All a bit gory, eh? But a hitman has to know his trade inside out or he won't last long.

Gold came up the stairs and put her gun away when she saw the scene.

'He's on his own, no others.' She had two garden waste bags under her arm.

'Quick thinking,' I complimented her as I took and unfolded them.

'Not really – bound to be a body up here, either his or yours.' She arched her eyebrows as I smiled. Cheeky bitch.

We parcelled our man up and I went to my office for some gaffer tape. The cleaners had done a good job; even the bullet hole in the plasterboard wall was filled and blended with the right plasterboard colour, and the toilet had a new door. The lino or whatever it's called nowadays was clean as a new pin, and the whole place still had a slight smell of bleach. I locked up, and between us we carried the patent body bag down to the boot of my car. I called the magicians. It rang twice and a gruff voice answered.

'Seems like you are quite busy, Mr Nevis?'

'Just a single passenger this time,' I said.

'Ten o'clock, don't be late.'

'Do I get a discount for three?'

The phone went dead; seems I don't.

All went smoothly at the magicians again that night. Foggy and Clegg aren't exactly brilliant conversationists; a grunt and a nod when I handed over the money was the full extent of the repartee. I arranged to meet Gold at the office car park late the next morning and we'd take a look at River's house. I had a plan of how I would get a look inside.

****

CHAPTER 10

Deptford Scrap Metals, Buyers of Ferrous and Non-ferrous Metals, is a half-acre plot at the back of the Deptford industrial estate in South London. I pulled in and parked up in one of three parking spaces marked *visitors* outside the portacabin office. It was actually marked *visiters*; primary education in Deptford has never been that good. The site was busy, as mobile cranes pulled written-off cars from a five deep row and dropped them into a crusher. The cubes of metal that emerged after crushing were lifted onto a row of six deep cubes, waiting to be hauled off and loaded onto a freighter at the docks on their way overseas. The whole operation was slick and run by Annie Greggs, a chain-smoking cockney lady; the epitome of mutton dressed as lamb. Pushing seventy, she had a blonde wig, make-up she must put on with a trowel, duck lips, Botox cheeks, tight tank top, breast implants to shame Dolly Parton, and wore miniskirts, fishnet stockings and high heel boots. How could you not love her?

She'd inherited the yard from her father, who somehow ended up in his own crusher. She'd always maintained he'd slipped on the edge when a gear got stuck and he was trying to release it; others say he welshed on a debt to somebody he shouldn't have and paid the price. I don't know the truth, but I do know that Annie is good at what she does; she doesn't suffer fools, and has been known to lay out a heavy docker who ridiculed her appearance with just one right-hander. She and I go back a few years.

She was sitting behind the long counter and looked up from a glossy fashion magazine she was reading when I entered.

'Don't tell me, it's Vogue and they've done a centre spread on you, Annie!' I quipped as she looked up.

'Fuck you, Nevis.' The lady has style. A broad smile crossed her face. 'Ben Nevis, well, well, well, what brings you here? Have you decided to accept my open offer of holy matrimony, or do you want some crime covered up in the crusher?'

Her security man sat in an old armchair reading the paper, and her current toy-boy, who looked about eleven, sat in another one fiddling on his phone. I knew the security man from when he ran the door at various London nightclubs; we exchanged nods.

'I'd love to marry you, Annie, but I don't think I could stay the pace,' I leant across the counter and gave her a peck, taking care not to dislodge the cheap blonde wig. 'Business call only, I'm afraid.'

She closed the magazine and sighed. 'Oh well, I can only hope. Right, what are you after then?'

'I need a car, a runner – no markings and a false plate.' By no markings I meant that all the registration numbers engraved on the engine and chassis would have been filed off. I knew Annie would have a few waiting to be crushed as drug dealers use them. You're not going to travel around London delivering kilos of coke in a traceable car with a genuine number plate; they use one for a few deliveries and then swap it for another at Annie's or some other scrapyard. It's good business for them. 'And it won't be coming back,' I added.

'Follow me.' She came round the counter and I followed a pair of fishnets in high heels out of the portacabin, across the yard, and round behind the huge stacks of freezer cabinets, metal pipes and other various metallic cast-offs to a row of cars: the runners.

'Any preference?' Annie waved a hand over the row. 'All runners, all cleaned.' Cleaned meaning the registration marks had been filed off.

I settled on a six year-old, according to the false number plate, BMW. BMWs are heavy cars, and I wanted a heavy car for what I had in mind. It had obviously had a smash at some time, with a bonnet that was a bit lopsided and some amateur paint spraying of the passenger side doors that wasn't even a near match to the original. I pointed at it. 'Just the job.'

'Two grand.'

I couldn't argue; she would get five hundred a week to rent it to a dealer, and I'd told her it wouldn't be coming back, so that was fair. I didn't have to be told it was 'cash only'; everything with Annie was 'cash only', and I had called into the bank before driving over to refill my ankle money pouch and take another three for Annie's bill, so two was okay. We did the exchange in the office, car keys for cash. I arranged with Annie that she'd hide my Range Rover round the back until I came back to pick it up and drove the BMW back to my office carpark. Gold was already there, sitting in her Lexus.

'Upgraded the motor then,' she remarked. 'Two tone as well.'

I ignored it and gave her River's house postcode that I'd written down in Clancy's office.

'That's River's house – put it in your sat nav and lead the way.' The journey was trouble free. I was pretty sure that if I'd met up with any police cars they'd have pulled me over. Their ANPR is continually on clocking number plates on the roads, but we made it to the delightful village of Whittington in the Cotswolds and then out of it on country roads until Gold pulled into a layby. I joined her in her car and accepted a hot coffee from her thermos. She thinks of everything.

'Any biscuits?'

'Piss off.' Well, not everything. 'The house is about a quarter of a mile up the road. I take it you are going to ram the gates with the BMW?'

'Yes, that's the idea, and then get inside amongst the confusion. But not until it's dark.'

Well, that was the plan, but it didn't work out that way. Woodward was on the mobile just as I settled down for forty winks.

'I'm at GCHQ, bit of a game in the night,' he said. 'In house radar picked up a drone coming in high and then flying down and hovering over an open courtyard. Take a look.'

A video flicked up on the mobile screen. It was a pretty clear picture of the drone hovering. It was a professional bit of kit with a camera, and more interestingly it had a hanging cord with a canvas bag on the end. It hovered, the camera moved around, and then it flew off

Woodward continued. 'It didn't pick up anything, probably because whoever was supposed to drop something into the bag was put off by the security chaps watching it.'

'There's a camera, the drone operator could have seen them,' I ventured. 'You think it was sent for the box?'

'Yes, most probably had a rendezvous booked for a pick up. Anyway, it flew off again empty-handed and the box is still where it should be. It could have been the way they got the box out before, so I think they'll try again. Get yourself up here, I've got a plan.'

I just hoped it wasn't a Baldrick-type 'cunning plan' like Woodward's last one that had me hiding in prickles and being shot at. I told Woodward where we were, and that we'd be with him inside an hour. I didn't bother telling him of my plan with the BMW, and we set off for Cheltenham.

****

CHAPTER 11

The centre of GCHQ is a grass-covered courtyard used for recreation, and where employees can sit and have their sandwiches or pot noodles in good weather.

The weather was good, and the Head of GCHQ Security, Commander Weeks, Woodward, Gold and myself stood at the doorway from the building into the courtyard. It was empty but for a few staff taking a break.

'We get quite a few idiots flying their drones over us, mainly kids with their birthday present. We can send out a signal that cuts off their signal and it drops to earth.' Commander Weeks was young for a Commander; the insignia was naval, so I presume the Navy had precedence on the security, as most of the UK's defence and retaliation would be through nuclear submarines and warships. 'We even have them turning up at the gatehouse with mum asking for it back. No chance.' He laughed.

I liked Weeks. He was obviously the ideal man for the job: no heart, and doesn't take prisoners.

Woodward spoke. 'Looking at the video of the drone it's a professional job, not one of Commander Weeks's child toys, so I think whoever is operating it will try again. Especially if they had success before.'

'If they had success before, how come the radar didn't pick it up that time?' I asked.

'Not looking for it,' Weeks answered. 'Our radar is looking for enemy attack aircraft and missiles – the whole of Cheltenham and a five mile surrounding airspace is a no-fly zone. The radar is looking up for incoming, not for drones at ground level sneaking over the buildings. They've put a ground radar in now.'

'So why wasn't last night's pick up a success?'

'No rendezvous made – whoever was supposed to meet it didn't. Either they couldn't get the box, or they noticed Commander

Weeks's men watching the drone,' explained Woodward.

'They couldn't get the box,' said Weeks. 'Since the theft we've stepped up security in that section. New CCTV covers the code desk. My guess is that whoever had planned to take the box last night and hook it onto the drone didn't know about the new camera until they got near the desk and saw it. Then they aborted the operation. It's a busy room, and looking at other CCTV there's a lot of our staff walking near that desk, all perfectly entitled to be there. Our would-be thief is probably one of them, but impossible to say which one.'

'Why didn't you bring the drone down like the others?'

'I told him not to,' said Woodward. 'Commander Weeks called me as soon as they spotted that it was a few grades above the normal children's type drone, and as no contact with anybody here was made I asked him to let it go in the hope they try again. I told you, we have a plan. We intend to make it easy for the box to be taken from the code desk, apprehend the thief, load the drone as though all was well, and track it back to its base.'

'River's house,' I said.

'Maybe, but we need to be sure.'

'How are you going to make it easy for the box to be taken?'

'When the in-house radar picks up the drone coming in, there will be a power failure in the code room. Lights out, which will spur the thief on to go for the box.'

'How will you know if somebody takes it if the lights are out?'

'The new camera is night sight.'

Clever.

****

We sat in Weeks's office in front of a wall of CCTV camera screens that evening and well into the night. No drone.

GCHQ has an overnight visitor area with five hotel type rooms: bed, bath, tea maker and telly. They gave us one each. I took Gold into Cheltenham for lunch the next day after we'd had a good rest and sleep. It was nice to relax for a while; mind you, watching how quickly Gold went through money at various boutiques and clothes shops, I wouldn't be relaxed if I was her other half. But as far as I know, there is no *significant other* in her life.

The thought kept crossing my mind that perhaps Woodward was wrong, perhaps River and his Chinese friends had had enough. Perhaps River was getting worried that the trail was leading towards him and didn't fancy a long prison sentence. If he was having misgivings, he was persuaded away from them the second night.

The call from the radar operations room came at one in the morning as we sat patiently in Weeks's office. The ground radar had picked up a drone skirting the wall and then coming in low over the roof.

'Showtime.' Weeks stood and gave orders to the security men seated in front of their screens. 'Cut all lights in the code room – flicker them like a power cut and then cut them.'

We watched the screens as the ones with cameras in the code room blacked out; all except the one with the night-sight camera. It went deep green, with various lighter patches caused by heat from the code desk and computers above it. Human shapes passed across the screen as the staff left the room, as was the standard procedure with any outage or emergency; they would wait in an allocated assembly place until power was restored.

The screen was static for a short while, and then a human form appeared and loitered by the desk.

'Got you.' Weeks said it softly, and then loudly he instructed his security men, 'LIGHTS!'

The lights in the code room flickered on, and the cameras picked up a startled man with the box in his hands, not knowing whether to put it back or run. He had his mind made up for him as security men in full operational uniform kit and carbines pointing at him came into view. We couldn't hear anything, but the man sank to the floor with hands behind his head, presumably on the orders of the security men.

'Who is he, do we know?' asked Woodward.

'No – will do soon though, he'll have a pass and ID.' Weeks ordered his men to take the man to the Security Area and hold him there.

'Right, part two then, come on.' Woodward led us out of the room and along a corridor until we reached the exit door for the courtyard. 'Here…' He took a block of wood roughly the same size as the code box from his coat and passed it to me. 'Put that in the drone's bag and keep your face from view as you do. It's pretty dark out there, so you should be okay. There's a tracker screwed into the bottom.'

Woodward's 'cunning plan' might just work. I took the box and switched the tracker on. It had just a very small green LED light that flashed, showing it was operating. Hanging below the drone, it wouldn't be in the view of the camera.

I stepped out into the courtyard. I couldn't see the drone; had its camera picked up something not right and they'd aborted the pick-up? I couldn't see it, but I could hear the soft swirling of its three helicopter blades in the darkness above me. I walked out into the open with my head bent forward. They must have seen me as the drone lowered into view to my side and hovered twenty feet above, with the bag dangling at head height. It didn't take more than a few seconds to slip the block inside, and I scampered back to the dark edge of the courtyard as the drone held its place for a few moments and then rose up and away over the building.

Inside the corridor, Weeks had the tracker signal showing on a map on a laptop. 'All good, got a good signal.'

'Not for long.' Woodward was worried.

'Come on, let's get after it before it goes out of range.

We ran after Weeks through the myriad of corridors to the staff exit, where a blacked-out Transit of the West Mercia Police ARV unit waited, complete with eight AR Officers in full combat gear, pistols and carbines. We scrambled in and wedged between them; something Gold no doubt enjoyed.

Woodward answered my question before I even asked it. 'Can't use Weeks's security people, they only have legal jurisdiction within the doughnut confines.'

Gold pulled my PKK from her ever present shoulder bag and gave it to me with two 12 shot clips of 9mm bullets. Woodward frowned and arched his eyebrows at that.

'I seem to remember you gave me two objectives for this job,' I reminded him, arching my eyebrows back at him. 'Find out how they got the box out of GCHQ, which we now know, and one other thing?'

No reply, but he knew what I was saying.

Weeks was up front beside the driver, directing him from the tracker's signal on the laptop. Both Gold and myself knew where we would end up. And we did; River's house.

I got dropped off at the layby where I'd left the BMW. The Transit went on with lights out to River's house and stopped before being in sight of the cameras at the gate. I had to smile when I saw the 'Police Aware' sticker on the BMW windscreen. I pulled it off and drove towards River's place, pulling up alongside the Transit.

'I'll smash through the gates and you can follow me in,' I told the AR in charge.

He nodded. 'Okay, I'll leave two of my men at the gate and the rest will secure the house and grounds. When you smash through the gates, pull off the drive as our vehicle will go straight to the house. Ready when you are.' And he got back into the Transit.

I nodded that I understood, although I intended to go for the house as well if the wheels were still on the BMW after I'd crashed the gates. I drove past the gates and did a U-turn a couple of hundred metres up the lane, then hit the accelerator, going up through the gears as my speed quickly picked up to seventy. As I came near the gates I took to the far side of the road and swung across and into them, as dead centre as I could to hit the place of least resistance.

The gates offered less resistance than I thought they would; digital locks don't hold firm like a good old fashioned heavy chain and padlock. They bounced off the front of the BMW as it hit them, opening out like a butterfly's wings, and hit the stone walls of the gateway on either side before bouncing back against the side of the car, leaving a dent and wide scratch along the rear doors. I kept my foot down towards River's mansion a hundred metres in front of me, all lit up by ground floodlights on the lawn either side of the drive. My rear view mirror reflected the blast of light from the ARV's headlights into my eyes as it roared behind me. The drone and its fake box with the tracker had obviously been found and was causing panic amongst some at the house. River's car was parked on the front gravel courtyard with two Range Rovers, and was being loaded with boxes and cases by four people. It looked like they were expecting us and were getting ready to flee.

The first Range Rover's driver decided to make a run for it over the lawn and hit the accelerator, sending a shower of gravel over the others who bent away from it, shielding their faces. I swung the BMW round off the drive, across the grass and hit the Range Rover's front offside wheel arch. Range Rovers aren't good at staying upright,t and this one tipped over and slithered on the grass like a slowly twisting curling stone for a few metres before coming to a rest. I pulled up twenty metres away and waited. The driver's door was now on top and was pushed open as the driver scrambled out and jumped down onto the grass. His first shot shattered the BMW windscreen. Why had I not thought of that? Stupid assumption that it would be bullet proof. He had nowhere to go. I don't know where his second shot went, but my first fired through the hole where the windscreen used to be split his heart in two, broke a rib, and exited his back before his body hit the ground.

Behind me at the house, the AROs had shot out the floodlights and met no resistance from the other three men who were laid flat on the ground, their hands secured behind their backs by strong plastic ties. River wasn't amongst them.

'Couldn't you have taken him prisoner?' asked Woodward, looking over to the corpse beside the upturned Range Rover as I approached.

'It was him or me,' I said. 'I preferred it to be him.'

'These three aren't saying anything, won't say who's in the house if anybody.' Woodward nodded to the three on the ground. 'Chinese Embassy staff, so no doubt we will have to hand them over. Diplomatic immunity.'

'Could hand them over dead.'

'I'm not in the execution business, Nevis,' he rebuked me.

'You were in Afghanistan,' I reminded him.

Woodward looked at me and nodded. 'Different situation.'

He had been my CO during my days in N14, the elite SAS unit that penetrated the Al Qaeda hideouts in the Tora Bora Mountains and called in air strikes on their commanders. His career path from there had taken him into the top echelon of MI6 where I had also moved to, and we parted when I left to go private, only to bump into each other again a couple of years later when a private job I was involved in turned into a national security one that he was also involved in, and since then when any *red label* work came his way he sought me out; r*ed label* work being jobs where, *if you are caught, the British Government does not know you, has never heard of you, and most certainly won't support you in any way...* work that suits me and pays well, having been trained to kill, and most *red label* work does involve a bit of that when necessary to achieve a result. Too many with my training who leave that domain of work, be it private or in the Services, suffer terribly with mental problems. You can hand your uniform back, but not your mindset. Do you really think a serviceman having done a few tours in the Middle East, being shot at, avoiding IEDs and with the threat of capture and being beheaded 24/7 can go and flip burgers in a McDonalds?

'Here, Gold said to give you these.' Woodward handed me an ear piece, clip mic and belt battery pack for them and a pair of night vision glasses with an elastic back grip. 'She went off round the side in the dark.'

Like me, Gold had noticed the absence of River who we knew to be in the mansion and had gone off to find him. I snapped the battery pack on my belt, put the ear piece in and clipped the mic onto my collar and plugged it all together.

'Keep the AROs here whilst I go inside and find River,' I said to Woodward.

'We don't want any friendly fire incidents.'

He knew what I had in mind if I found River; no point in wasting taxpayers' money on a long trial and then a long custodial sentence. Woodward said nothing and kept his own counsel, but he knew why I didn't want any AROs inside with me. I didn't want any witnesses.

'Nevis to Gold,' I called her.

'I'm doing a reccy round the back,' she said.

'Anything?'

'Not yet.'

'River has to be inside somewhere.'

'Yeah, what do you want to do?'

'Create a diversion at the back and I'll slip in the front.'

'Will do, on the count of ten.'

I counted under my breath and ran to the front of the house, flattening myself against the stone wall beside a pair of large French doors. Precisely on the ten count, a sharp explosion echoed from the back of the house; Gold had thrown the grenade inside. I stepped in front of the French doors and kicked them in, moving inside and to the right so I wouldn't show up against the moonlight outside if anybody was inside. Nobody was. I slipped down my night visions; the room was a large sitting room, plenty of expensive furniture. It had two doors, one on the left that would lead to the entrance hall, and one off to the back rooms. I took the one to the hall and slipped through it, just in time to see somebody disappear at the top of a wide staircase that wound up from the large open hall to the first floor. I could smell smoke; Gold's grenade must have set the place on fire. A door on the left of the hall opened and somebody came out; night visions pick up body heat and show green to white patches depending on the amount of heat. Green is the usual body temperature indicator. This green shape was definitely a body and halted when it saw me; a spurt of white light midway down the body meant the bastard had fired at me, and missed. I dropped to the floor and put two bullets into him. The green shape collapsed on the floor and remained still. I moved over and raised my night visions to get a better look; hopefully it was River. It wasn't, it was another Chinese foot soldier; probably another cultural attache at the Embassy – how many were they allowed? His gun had clattered away when he fell, but he still held Woodward's block of wood in his hand and the LED was still flashing. He must have been sent to collect what River thought was the code box from the drone when it landed in the grounds. The others on their faces in the front were probably part of that search party, and when they'd seen the wood block and tracker they knew the game was up, and were loading the cars ready to flee. River would have a surprise when given a block of wood. Didn't matter now, as the carrier of bad news was dead; my second shot had gone through his right eye and into his brain. I left him and moved up the stairs as silently as I could; thick carpet made that easier. It must have been River who I had seen at the top. The top of the staircase led out to the end of a long corridor with three rooms off each side. This was dodgy; clearing rooms of enemy personnel is a specialist job for two trained people. One person entering a room is a sitting duck. I could do with a couple of stun grenades, but I didn't have any. What I did have was a selection of vases on a side table in the corridor. They were probably very expensive antiques, but needs must.

I picked a small one up, and at the first door I kicked it open; and moving back against the corridor wall beside it, I rolled the vase in along the floor at speed. Anybody inside in the dark would think it was a grenade and panic, hopefully rushing out. The vase smashed against something, but nobody fled out. Next vase, next room, same result: empty. The third room paid dividends; when the vase went in, a loud scuffling inside told me somebody was battening down behind a chair or something else for cover. They wouldn't be watching the door, they'd be sheltering from a flash and a bang, so I slipped inside and sank to my knees against the wall. The night visions showed an amount of green light beside a dark object: somebody was hiding. I shot at the green and a shout of agony told me I'd scored a hit. No firing came back at me. I stood and ran my hand up the wall, head height, beside the left side of the door frame, the place where you usually find the light switch. I did, and two hanging bulbs in round shades lit the room. It was a bedroom, a big bedroom with an en-suite bathroom off it. Groans were coming from behind a button back armchair which complemented a similar sofa. I went over and kicked it over onto its side, revealing Desmond River on his knees nursing a smashed elbow where my bullet had hit him. He turned and looked up at me. His eyes widened in recognition.

'You!'

'Yes, 'fraid so.' We had never met, so that confirmed that the Chinese had a photo of me.

'You should be dead.'

'Yeah, lots of people have said that. Most of them are dead themselves now. Like your friend Erskin Powell.'

River laughed. 'Erskin? He was a fool, one of those idiots that think they can change the world by sharing military secrets amongst the major powers. He was just a mule – useful, but stupid. Politicians are able to move country to country with their diplomatic bags. No Customs, no searches.'

'To be dispensed with when you feel like it, eh? Like his brother?'

'He was a fool too. We had a deal with Erskin, and then he brought in his brother who threatened to expose us unless he got a lot more money. I don't like threats, Mr Nevis. I don't like people pointing a gun at me either. You aren't going to pull the trigger.'

'No, why not?'

I felt the cold steel of a gun barrel press against the back of my neck.

'Because my wife will shoot you if you do, so lower your gun.'

I lowered it and a hand reached around and took it. The barrel left my neck and I turned to see Sun Zalny pointing a gun at me, and she was smiling.

River raised himself, groaning with the pain from his elbow.

Sun Zalny spoke. 'Such a shame, Mr Nevis. All that trouble and we have the code box after all, and you are going to die,' she said in perfect English. 'Your country's satellite defence system will be breached, and you will be open to missile attacks. They won't come from China, Mr Nevis, of course not – too obvious. We will make every terrorist organisation that hates the West aware that their missiles would not be destroyed en route. North Korea and the Iranian Revolutionary Guard will pay billions for that chance. A brilliant idea, do you not agree? Such a shame you won't be here to see the destruction.'

I needed time; where are you, Gold? 'You don't have the code box,' I said with a false smile. 'You have a block of wood. GCHQ knew of your plan and arrested your man on the inside before he could put the box in the drone's bag. I put a block of wood with a tracker on it inside the bag. How do you think we followed it here so quickly?'

'You're lying.' She spat the words out. 'Come on, Desmond, we have to go – the car is waiting at the back gates. My men will have the code box.' She started to raise the gun.

I had one last card to play for time. Time to let Gold get here.

'The men you sent into the grounds to retrieve the box are in custody at the front of the house, except for one who tried to run and met with a fatal car accident. Another is laying dead at the foot of the stairs clutching a block of wood, not a code box, go and see for yorself.'

River struggled towards the door, clasping his broken arm to his body. 'Check it.'

She waved me out into the corridor with her gun and they followed me as we walked towards the stairs. The smoke was getting quite thick coming up the stairs, and flames from the fire in the back rooms lit the hall. From the top of the stairs we could see the goon I'd shot lying on the tiles, his motionless hand clutching the wooden block.

'Shit!' River could see it too.

I waited for death. I hoped Sun Zalny was a good shot. One to the head, please. I heard the crack of gunfire behind me. I was still standing; was she that bad a shot? I turned and Sun Zalny was spread out on the floor on her back, with blood seeping out of the exit wound in her forehead. River was leant against the stair banister with a look of shock on his face. Gold stood five metres down the corridor, her PKK raised and pointing at River. I don't know how many times over the years I've told myself that Gold is the best back-up in the business, just trust her; but she is, and I do.

'You left that late,' I said.

'Not at all,' she smiled. 'I had you covered from when the first hundred thousand pound Ming vase rolled into a room and smashed. That was an expensive trick, Ben. What do you want to do with him?'

I looked at River and remembered Woodward's second objective of the operation. 'Accident,' I said. Moving beside him and cupping my right arm behind his legs, I lifted fast and over the banister he went, falling like a sack of spuds and thudding into the tiled hallway twenty metres below, 'An unfortunate accident.' I bent and picked up my gun which had fallen from Zalny's hand. 'Come on, let's go.'

By the time we had got to the bottom of the staircase the fire had really taken hold and the smoke was pouring into the hall. We left quickly and joined Woodward on the front lawn. The AROs were moving back in case the whole place toppled over.

'Fire brigade on their way?' I shouted at Woodward over the cracking of the massive roof timbers and falling masonry hitting the steps and courtyard.

'Not yet.'

It was obvious he wanted the whole place to go up in flames and destroy any evidence that we'd been here, so the brigade hadn't been called and wouldn't be called. If somebody from the local village saw a glow in the sky and rang them, it would be a good half hour before they got here.

'River and Sun Zalny are dead,' I shouted.

'Good. Come on, let's get out of here. Is that car driveable?' He pointed to the BMW.

'Yes, just about.' Its front passenger wing was gone, severed when I hit the Range Rover side-on, but it was still a 'runner'.

Woodward walked over to the ARO in charge and had a few words. Two AROs were quickly despatched to pick up the dead body by the Range Rover and manhandle it to the burning building, where they moved inside with it and came scurrying out without it. Woodward came back over to us.

'All the bodies are inside, and with a bit of luck the fire will burn them to nothing and the building collapse on top of them. Where did you throw the grenade in?' He looked at Gold.

'Kitchen.'

'Good, accidental fire then – somebody left a frying pan on the gas.' He smiled. 'Come on, let's go back to GCHQ – and get that BMW out of here too.'

Gold and I went to the BMW and manhandled the front wing into the back seat as the ARV left. We got in.

'I've got an interesting picture.' Gold reached into the shoulder bag and pulled out a photo. 'I found this on the mantelpiece in the back lounge when I got into the house.' She passed it over.

It was the Rivers' wedding photo. Usual set up, bride and groom; River and Sun Zalny surrounded by family, all hers by the look of it, taken in a grove of flowering cherry trees in full blossom. 'What am I looking at?' I knew there would be something that Gold had noticed.

'Standing at the back, right-hand side, head and shoulders.'

I looked, and there he was: the Chinaman, the eye patch a give-away.

'Interesting,' I said.

'He certainly moves in high Chinese society – you'd have to be pretty important to get an invite to the wedding of a Politburo member's daughter.'

I slammed the car into gear and we made our way out onto the lane, wondering just who this Chinaman was.

****

In Weeks's office back at GCHQ, Woodward looked at the wedding photo.

'He's got grade one security clearance.'

'Burgess, Philby and Maclean had that too,' I reminded him.

'How often does he visit?' Woodward asked Weeks.

'Usually once a month, sometimes more – he's got MOD clearance for the Code Room and that's it. He can't wander around.'

'Is he accompanied by security when he's here?' I asked.

'No.'

'Then he could wander around.'

Weeks shook his head. 'No, he only gets the swipe card for the Code Room – all departments have their own swipe card entry security.'

Woodward leant back, steepled his fingers and thought for a few moments before making a decision. 'Okay, we keep this amongst ourselves. Nevis, you have a good look into him, let's see what you can find. Softly, softly though, he could be a bona fide UK agent and have infiltrated the Chinese to that level.'

'Or he could be a Chinese agent who's infiltrated your lot.' I got one in on Woodward; doesn't often happen. 'Has he got a name?'

'Zang Wei.' He spelt it out as Gold noted it on her mobile.

'What about this chap who tried to get the box to the drone, has he said anything?' I addressed Weeks.

'Not a lot – lives local, been with us for four years, university graduate, and is shit scared of going to prison.'

'Politically motivated?' I asked.

'No, he says he was blackmailed after a night with a girl in a hotel – typical honey trap. He had some pictures sent to him by email the next day that had been doctored and showed him *in flagrante* with underage kids, and a threat of sending them to his family and to us unless he did what he was told. His instructions were sent online – he was given the day and time the drone would be there, so he could swap a shift with another of the staff and make sure he got the code box out to it.'

'I bet Zang Wei picked him out during his visits to the Code Room. Single bloke, good job and career, he wouldn't want to lose that.'

'He has now,' Weeks commented.

'Okay,' Woodward sighed. 'We won't get any more out of him, so full speed ahead on Zang Wei.'

****

Weeks offered Gold and myself the overnight visitor's accommodation at GCHQ again, but I like my own bed and at that time in the night there's not much traffic about, so I followed her Lexus back to London on the A roads as far as we could. Motorway cameras would have picked us up and noted the BMW with no MOT, no tax, no owner and no insurance, and sent a patrol car to pull me over and probably put me in a cell for the night. Not the ideal end to the day.

I parked the BMW in the underground car park at my apartment block and wandered up to collect my keys from the security chaps at the desk in the foyer. I could see from their smiles that I was in for some banter.

'Going into stock car racing, Mr Hadlow?' was the first bit. They had seen me park the BMW on their CCTV screens.

'Wouldn't it be better parked out by the bins, sir?' came next.

I swapped some banter back and explained that it was a prop in a film I was involved with. My false references for the landlords when I rented the apartment were that I was in the media: documentary films.

I collected my keys, picked up a service charge invoice, the bane of all who live in London apartments, and took the lift to my floor, showered, and fell into bed.

****

CHAPTER 12

Woodward wanted a meet; he was on the mobile at nine the next morning interrupting my coffee, bran flakes and walnuts. I arranged to meet him at the Concourse cafe at eleven, much to his disgust, but I thought the office might still be a place to avoid as I may still be a target after last night. I called Gold to ask her to be there too. She wasn't happy.

'I'm busy.'

'Personal?' I guessed she had a 'gold digger' client due.

'No, business/ Zang Wei.'

'Go on.' I was intrigued.

'Well, I thought it through, and if he is with the CMS then last night's happenings would have sent a shock through their UK organisation – and with some of their men killed and the box theft a failure, my past dealings with them tells me Zang is going to be in trouble. They don't like failure. He's either going to be on a flight home or carpeted, so I'm sitting on the plinth by the Stuart White statue in Portland Square acting like a tourist – it gives me a great view of the entrance to the Chinese Embassy, so if Zang goes in and comes out I can follow him. Unless he goes in and doesn't come out, then he's a *goner*.'

Well, if he was a '*goner*', that would save me the trouble.

∗∗∗∗∗∗∗∗∗∗∗∗∗∗∗∗∗∗∗∗∗∗

I took an Uber to Charing Cross. Woodward made a great play as usual of flipping his leather gloves over the Concourse cafe seat before lowering his fawn Crombie onto it.

'Coffee?' I offered. Only polite to offer.

The look of utter disdain gave me his usual answer.

'Would your two chaps like a cup?' I asked, nodding towards his bodyguards who were seated behind us trying not to look like an inconspicuous pair of heavy bookends.

He ignored the offer. 'I wanted to bring you up to date, Nevis.'

He had briefed the Foreign Secretary, who was calling in the Chinese Ambassador to ask for an explanation as to how Chinese diplomatic cars were found at a burned down English country house belonging to a well-respected British businessman and his wife who could not be traced? Nothing would be said about bodies inside, as the Home Office forensic unit would be doing that work, not the local police forensic unit, as they were not covered by the Official Secrets Act.

If the Chinese Ambassador knew River's wife, Sun Zalny, was the daughter of a Politburo member, which he probably did, and if he knew she was dead, he would quickly be landing the blame on a scapegoat to save his own skin; that scapegoat would be Zang Wei.

It was all smoke and mirrors, like most diplomatic spats. Both sides knew exactly what was going on, but neither side would admit it. A Defence and Security Media Advisory Notice,

DSMA for short, had been put on the fire with the media; that's an updated version of the old fashioned D Notice, and bans any mention of something in the news, in this case the fire at River's house.

Woodward shifted a little closer to me. 'As far as MI6 is concerned, Nevis, the whole episode is now closed and filed with a twenty year lock on it.' He paused to underline his next words. 'As far as *you* are concerned, the objective spoken about before is ongoing.'

He still wanted Zang Wei killed.

'Okay.'

'No contact until complete.'

And with that he stood, made another show of flicking his leather gloves over the back of his Crombie, gave a curt nod and left the cafe. His two bodyguards followed a few metres behind.

I finished the coffee; it was awful, but you couldn't use the Concourse cafe and not buy something to eat or drink. The antidote to British Rail coffee is a strong mint, and I had a roll in my pocket. There is no antidote to a British Rail sandwich. My mobile buzzed. It was Gold.

'Got him.'

'You have?'

'Yes, he must have been in the Embassy early – he left about ten minutes ago and got a cab. I'm following, seems to be going into the West End. I'll give you a call when we get to wherever it is he's heading for.'

She clicked off. I called an Uber and went back home to pick up the BMW; it was where I'd left it, security hadn't moved it out to the bins. Cheeky buggers. The small strip of sellotape was still in place where I'd put it over the door and body work, and a similar piece still in place over the edge of the boot door and body work; nobody had been in the car. I laid down and checked underneath; no magnetic IEDs either. All clear. I hadn't expected anything, but that routine is impressed into my brain like *clunk-click* every trip is. I was pulling out of the car park when Gold called with an update.

'It's the Lotus Flower, he's inside.'

'Okay, I'll come over. Where are you?'

'Fifty metres down the road parked on double yellows, so if a traffic warden turns up I'll go round the block and come back.'

'Okay.'

I made my way over and she was in the same spot. I parked behind and slipped into her passenger seat.

'Any movement?' I asked.

'No. I wandered past once to check he hadn't left by a back door, but he's still there having a meal.' She looked at me. 'You could just walk in and *bang bang*.' She formed her hand into a gun shape.

It wasn't a bad idea, but the staff had seen me once, and if they recognised me I wouldn't get past the door. Plus the street CCTVs would have picked me up by now, as well as the BMW, although that was untraceable.

My mobile rang. It was Memet's number from the restaurant; what would he want? I hadn't ordered a takeaway and forgotten.

'Memet, what can I do for you, sir?'

'Mr Nevis, you leave your gas on?'

I didn't understand. 'Did I do what?'

'The gas in your office, did you leave it on?'

'It's all electric Memet, no gas. Why?' I think I knew why.

'There's been an explosion and your office is wrecked. I ran up with others when it happened – the windows are all gone and everything inside all broken. Thank God you weren't there.'

'Yes, thank God I wasn't. What's happening now, Memet?'

'Fire brigade, police and ambulance are here.'

'Anybody hurt?'

'One man, he must be a customer of yours – he's alive but in a bad way. He was in the corridor by your office door and caught the full blast.'

'Chinaman?'

'Yes.'

'Nobody inside?'

'No.'

'Okay, thanks for that, Memet. I'm in Scotland, but I'll be back as soon as I can get a flight.' I lied. I wanted time to sort things out before I started answering police questions about how an all-electric office managed to blow up.

'Okay, I tell the police.'

I closed the phone and looked at Gold. 'You got the gist of that?'

'The bastards blew up your office.'

'And blew up their own bomber.'

'You still sure you don't want to go in the restaurant and *bang bang*?'

'Too late, look.' I pointed to the Lotus Flower; Zang was leaving. He hailed a passing black cab.

'Maybe he's going to take a look at your office.'

'If news has got back to the Embassy that Sun Zalny is dead, and now they've blown up one of their own, he's probably doing a runner. Keep on his tail, I'll follow.'

I jumped out of Gold's car and back into the BMW, pulling out into the traffic about ten cars behind her. Zang was heading south towards the Thames, so Gold could be right; he was going to my office, perhaps hoping I'd be there looking at the damage and he'd get a chance to finish me and recoup some points with the Embassy. But he didn't head for London

Bridge and the Borough; he hit the embankment and went towards Vauxhall. The MI6 building, known in the trade as Legoland because of its shape, is on the south side of the embankment at Vauxhall; it's the one they blew up in the Bond film *Skyfall*, but that was just fiction – didn't really happen; this is real. His plan hit me. I rang Gold.

'He's going to Legoland, he's after Woodward!' Of course he was; killing Woodward would wipe out all the mistakes he had made in the box caper. He must realise he was most likely doomed to be recalled to Bejing anyway, so why not add a bit of kudos by assassinating a top man in MI6? I rang Woodward on his direct mobile.

'I said no contact until objective complete, Nevis, so I hope it is?'

'Where are you?'

'In my office, why?'

'I think Zang is on his way to kill you.'

There was a short silence.

'He *is* on his way here, he called for a meeting earlier.'

'He blew up my office this morning, blowing up one of his own men at the same time – add that to Sun Zalny's death at Whittingbourne and he's in big trouble at home. One way to redeem his career, and save himself from a flight home and the wrath of the CSS, would be to knock off a top spy master – you. Don't meet him.'

Woodward got the picture. 'Okay, where are you?'

'On his tail with Gold.'

'I'll have him blocked at the door – he won't get in.'

I was right. Zang's cab turned over Vauxhall Bridge and then left to Legoland; he left the cab on the road outside MI6 headquarters, skipped through the slow traffic and up the slip road to the front of the building.

Gold signalled to turn across the oncoming traffic which, as usual, wouldn't let her through, so nearly having a head-on with a bus as she forced her way across, she drove in, followed by me.

Zang was already through the main doors when we stopped outside and jumped from our vehicles. I took my PKK from the glove compartment and noticed Gold had hers as well. Outside security officers were already on their way over, waving their hands to tell us we couldn't park there; they did an abrupt about turn when they saw the guns. We reached the reflective main doors. If Zang saw us from inside, we'd be sitting ducks. He did see us, snd two bullets hit the glass from the inside; it was bullet proof and they left a small dent, surrounded by a star of cracks. I pulled open one of the doors, staying behind it for protection, and peeped in at the reception area; Zang was either hiding or gone. A security office lay moaning on the floor, clutching his leg; another two sprawled face down across the desk from the back, not moving. The building is open plan; I looked up at the levels above that had frightened staff looking down from the open corridors. An alarm siren started to wail; that was good, I knew from when I worked there that not only would the alarm go off but all the staff would immediately return to their open plan offices, knowing that the security procedure would automatically lock the doors, keeping them safe inside, and the emergency lighting would come on.

Gold pointed to the lifts. 'Look.'

One was open on the ground floor and empty; the other was in use, floors one and two LEDs lit as it travelled up.

Zang would know Woodward's office was on the third floor, he'd been there before.

'Third floor,' I told Gold. 'You take the lift, I'll take the stairs in case he comes that way.'

On my way up, I passed a few people who had been on the stairs when the alarm sounded, and remembering their training had stayed put. They cowed against the wall when they saw me and my PPK.

'I'm one of the good guys, stay put,' I told them as I passed.

At the third floor the open plan office system finished, and the floor was a normal corridor and offices type. I took a minute to catch my breath; running up stairs takes it out of you. Perhaps I should have taken the lift and sent Gold up the stairs; she was ten years younger than me. I listened and then looked carefully round the corner and down the corridor. It was empty; both lifts were stationary and their doors open. I couldn't see Gold. I moved slowly along the corridor, hugging the wall; I remembered that Woodward's office was at the far end, or at least it was the last time I visited it a couple of years ago. I checked the lifts; both empty and both switched to attendant mode, which stopped them moving if called from another floor. Gold doesn't miss a trick. The door to Woodward's office was open, n o sound from inside. I reached round the doorway and slowly pushed the door open; nobody was hiding behind it, the room was empty. It was tidy too – no sign of a struggle, everything in place. Where was Woodward, and where was Zang?

'They're on the balcony.'

I nearly jumped out of my skin as Gold's quiet voice came from the doorway behind me.

'What balcony?' There was no exit to a balcony from this office.

She beckoned me to follow her and turned and walked down the corridor to the far end with me following. The last door was open; it wasn't an office door, it was a fire escape door with a push bar system. I could feel a draft coming through it. Gold nodded towards the balcony. 'They're out there. Zang was shouting threats to kill Woodward unless he gets asylum.'

'He won't get that.' I was sure Woodward wouldn't allow that. God knows how much damage Zang had done to UK security in his time as a double-turned spy, how much wrong information he'd given us, and how many UK operatives he'd given up to his spy masters in China. He had taken Woodward in as well, and there's no coming back from that.

I stopped and moved onto the balcony; it bristled with antennae and satellite dishes of all shapes and sizes. Looking between them, I could see Zang and Woodward standing beside the concrete surround at the front. Woodward's head was bleeding from a gash on the temple; Zang must have pistol whipped him at some point. Zang had a small pistol aimed at Woodward. If Zang didn't get what he wanted, Woodward was dead, no doubt about that; because with no asylum, his only chance was to get back to the Chinese Embassy having killed Woodward. That might keep him alive back in China. Maybe, depends on how the Politburo would view the killing of one of their member's daughters. Not well, that's for sure.

I could hear the commotion from the street below coming up and over the low balcony wall, police sirens, and no doubt ARVs in profusion. Zang would hear that and know his time was limited.

I waved Gold to circle round from the right and started to circle left. The satellite dishes gave good cover and I got within ten metres of the pair. I was behind Zang; he shouted at Woodward and hit him hard on the previous head wound. Woodward dropped to his knees, covering the wound with his hands. Zang held his gun with two hands and pointed it down at Woodward's head.

Two shots rang out, one from me and one from Gold. Both hit Zang in the head and travelled through it, passing each other on the way. The gun dropped from Zang's hand and his body dropped into a heap beside Woodward, who raised his face towards me.

'Took your bloody time, Nevis.'

Gratitude eh?

****

It amazed me how quickly the area was cleared and cleaned. Spick and Span have got competition! Zang's body went into a body bag which was removed from the balcony, the blood on the ground cleaned up, and we were ushered off the balcony and down the corridor to Woodward's office, all in a matter of minutes. It was obviously a well-practiced routine. Woodward explained that speed was important in these days of drones with cameras. The last thing MI6 wanted was a picture of Zang's body on the balcony hitting the news or papers.

Woodward wouldn't be wearing his brown trilby for a few days, not with the amount of bandaging the medical staff had swathed his head with; it wouldn't fit. Under that were six stitches holding his wound tight shut to heal. The doctor had told him he was lucky, if the blow had been struck a few centimetres to the left he would have lost his eye. I cheered him up by saying he could have had Zang's eye patch if he had. That didn't go down well. Gold smiled though.

Another person joined Woodward in conversation well out of earshot of myself and everybody else in the room. She was mid-thirties and very smart in a trouser suit, one of those ladies that have an aura of top business about them, confident and in control. She held most of the conversation and I got the impression that she was Woodward's senior. She left, flashing Gold and me a nice smile. No words, just a smile.

Woodward cleared the room and came over to where Gold and I were lounging on an expensive sofa. He pulled up a chair and leant forward.

'Right, things are moving fast. The Foreign Secretary has already had the Chinese Ambassador in and called a COBRA meeting. The Chinese have been asked to explain why they would send an assassin into MI6 to kill people, and why their diplomatic vehicles were found at River's house which had been intentionally razed to the ground, the whereabouts of him and his wife unknown. They're not, as you know – his and her burnt remains are under the wreckage, but we won't admit finding them yet, going to hold that for use if we need it at a later date. The fact is, we have the body of Zang, so they can't deny a member of their staff made an assassination attempt on a member of the UK Security Staff, so we have them on the back foot. The official response from them is a denial that Zang is on their staff and to suggest he is from a Triad drug gang that MI6 has brought down and that this was a failed revenge killing by them. It holds water as a way out for them, as we have indeed brought down a few Triad gangs in the last year or two, but they just spring up again. They also tend to murder each other, but not the security forces of the country they are operating in as that would bring down too much law enforcement heat on them. The bottom line is that we know it's the Chinese CSS trying to get hold of the Code Box and disrupt the satellite defence system, they know we know, and throwing out the Triad answer means they are in the slurry back home and have to keep their noses clean here or quite a few will be recalled. It also means that by denying Zang is one of theirs, they can't take his body back, so we have to get rid of that. When we do clear River's house of rubble, Sun Zalny's body, or what's left of it, will not be found.' He gave us a broad smile.

'And I haven't just had this conversation with either of you.'

'How are you going to square the press and media with what's happened?'

'That's the easy bit – it was a single terrorist attack, some young idiot radicalised online, we've used that story before. The IT people here will conjure up a false name, picture, profile and history of our supposed terrorist that will be on social media in a matter of hours – we release the name to the media and off they go, chasing pixels. It will make the headlines for a day or two and then disappear. That's the good thing about the British media – always after the next story so nothing lasts.'

'What about Zang?'

'His body has to disappear immediately, can't have anything getting out about him.'

I had an idea. 'Is there a back vehicle entrance here?'

'Of course, there's an underground car park. Why?'

'Have Zang's body bag taken down there and tell security to let in an old BMW with a wing missing.'

Woodward didn't ask questions; he was old school, what you don't know can't hurt you. He just shrugged. 'Okay.'

Gold and I went down to the reception area; it was pristine clean already, the door panels with bullet marks were being replaced, and the whole outside area had been cleared of traffic. Spick and Span would have to raise their game to get this contract! The situation was over, and pretty soon the place would be functioning as though nothing had happened.

'You need me to follow?' asked Gold as we walked towards the cars.

'No, I've just got the one call to make and that should tie everything up nicely.'

'Okay, give me a call if you need me – and watch your back.'

I gave a wave as she drove her Lexus out of the slip road. I didn't get a wave back, not even a look, but that was Gold all over. She didn't ask what I was going to do with Zang's body; not relevant to her, so why bother? The one thing I know about her is that if I need her, one phone call and she would be there. And that's about all I know about her, except her military past which crossed with mine; I don't know where she lives, whether she has a partner, what she likes and doesn't like, who she sees, if anybody. I don't need to know any of that; all I need to know is her phone number.

I drove the BMW round the block and through a large roller shutter in the back wall of Legoland that rolled down as soon as I was in. The car park was large, well-lit and pretty full. A plain clothed security man waved to me from one of the stairwells at the back and I drove over. There were two of them, and Zang's body bag was on the floor between them. Nobody spoke as I got out and opened the boot. It was obvious why I opened it, and they put the body bag inside and I closed it again. Not a word passed between us. I drove towards the roller shutter door and it rolled up, letting me out.

At least I was out of the west end traffic and south of the Thames, so my journey to Annie's scrap yard was quite quick.

****

CHAPTER 13

Annie was stood outside her portacabin office with one of her men. Leather mini skirt, red fishnets, suede knee boots, low cut blouse, cantilever bra and wearing a purple wig Mary Quant style – her that is, not the man. I pulled up next to her.

'Where's the wing?' was her greeting as she noticed the BMW was missing one.

'Hello, Annie, you look lovely today,' I lied.

She ignored the platitude. 'I'll charge you extra for a missing wing.'

'It's in the back.' I gave her a peck on the cheek and was nearly bowled over by the waft of whatever cheap black market perfume she'd drenched herself in. 'But I need a chat.'

I took her arm and moved her out of earshot of the man, who wandered off into the yard.

She looked at me in a suspicious way. 'A chat? I don't suppose it's a chat about getting a special marriage licence for this afternoon and being on the next flight to the Caribbean?'

'No, a business chat.'

'I'll hide my disappointment. Go on?'

'There's a package in the boot that needs to disappear.'

She smiled. 'Just like the old days, eh Ben?'

She was referring to my early private eye days when I worked for a few bad characters in the London criminal underbelly, and sometimes took out their competitors. It was before I had made the acquaintance of the *magicians* and Annie was the go-to person, with large vats of acid round the back of the yard that were used to take the paint and oil off car engines, leaving them looking new. They also devoured a body in twenty-four hours.

'I don't have the acid baths anymore, Ben – health and safety banned 'em'

We both laughed at that. Looks like I'm off to the *magicians* then.

She carried on. 'I have the crusher.'

'The crusher?'

'Yes. *You* might have gone legit, Ben, but there's still people who want to disappear other people. Leave it to me. There's a cost, of course.'

'Of course.'

She walked into the yard and called a couple of her workers over. After a brief chat they came and drove the BMW into the yard. She came back to me.

'Come inside and have a coffee whilst they remove the engine, won't be long. Engines don't crush, they have to be smelted down – can't put an engine in the crusher.'

We retired to the portacabin where yet another toy-boy sat on a sofa playing on his iPhone. He looked about fourteen and grunted a welcome. He looked the body builder type, chest and arms straining the tight vest.

'Nice bodywork, Annie,' I commented, nodding towards the lad.

She scoffed. 'Yes, but not a lot under the bonnet.'

I put on a brave face as I forced down a truly awful cup of coffee, whilst Annie spent the next ten minutes on the phone to her bookie placing a number of bets on the evening card at Catford dog track.

'I didn't know you were a gambler, Annie?' I made conversation when she'd finished.

'Well, I have to have something to do in the evenings, Ben.' She looked towards the lad. 'Post-coital conversation isn't exactly exhilarating, so I can tune in on the internet and watch my money go down the drain.' She laughed.

One of her men poked his head round the door. 'All done, boss.'

We left the cabin and walked with him into the main area of the yard. The BMW sat on the ground next to the crusher, no engine and no tyres. Annie waved to the driver of a magnetic crane who was shifting piles of mixed metal into a large ship container on the back of an artic. He dropped his pile into it and trundled the crane over to us, swinging the big magnetic disc over the BMW before dropping it onto it with a metallic thud. He lifted the car off the ground, swung it over the crusher and dropped it in. The man who had fetched us from the cabin pressed a large button on the control panel and the big jaws slowly and noisily closed over the BMW in an orderly fashion, crushing it into a twelve foot long by four foot square slab. At the press of another button, the metal slatted conveyor belt ferried it out of the crusher onto a platform extension. I half expected to see blood and body fluid oozing out, but there wasn't any.

'No blood?' I asked Annie.

'Crushed too tight, Ben – be hard even to get air in or out of that block.'

The magnetic crane picked up the block and lifted it onto a neat pile of similar blocks arranged five wide and ten high along the edge of the yard.

Annie waved a hand at them. 'They'll be picked up in the morning and on a container ship at the docks and away.'

'Away to where?' I asked.

'China, they can't get enough scrap at the moment.'

I had to stop myself laughing. Oh dear, Mr Zang, not exactly the homecoming you had planned.

END

Thank you for buying this book. If you enjoyed it please leave a review or rating on Amazon as that would mean an awful lot to me.

To see more books in this series and others, and to get updates on new releases check my website:

<u>www.barry-faulkner.com</u>

Whilst there you may also like to sign up to my newsletter and receive advance notice of new books, freebies, talks, Literary Festivals I attend and other interesting posts. You can unsubscribe at any time and it's all **FREE**!!

Take care and stay safe!

DCS Palmer books

1. Future Riches
2. The Felt Tip Murders
3. A Killer is Calling
4. Poetic Justice
5. Loot
6. I'm With The Band

7. Burning Ambition
8. Take Away Terror
9. Ministry of Death
10. The Bodybuilder
11. Succession
12. The Black Rose
13. Laptops Can Kill

Ben Nevis and the Gold Digger Series

1. Turkish Delight
2. National Treasure
3. Chinese Takeaway

London Crime 1930s-2021 (factual)

UK Serial Killers 1930-2021 (factual)

Bidder Beware (Comedy crime)

Fred Karno   biography

---

www.barry-faulkner.com

Printed in Great Britain
by Amazon